# AMPHIBIAN'S KISS

## ALL THAT GLITTERS

# LICHELLE SLATER

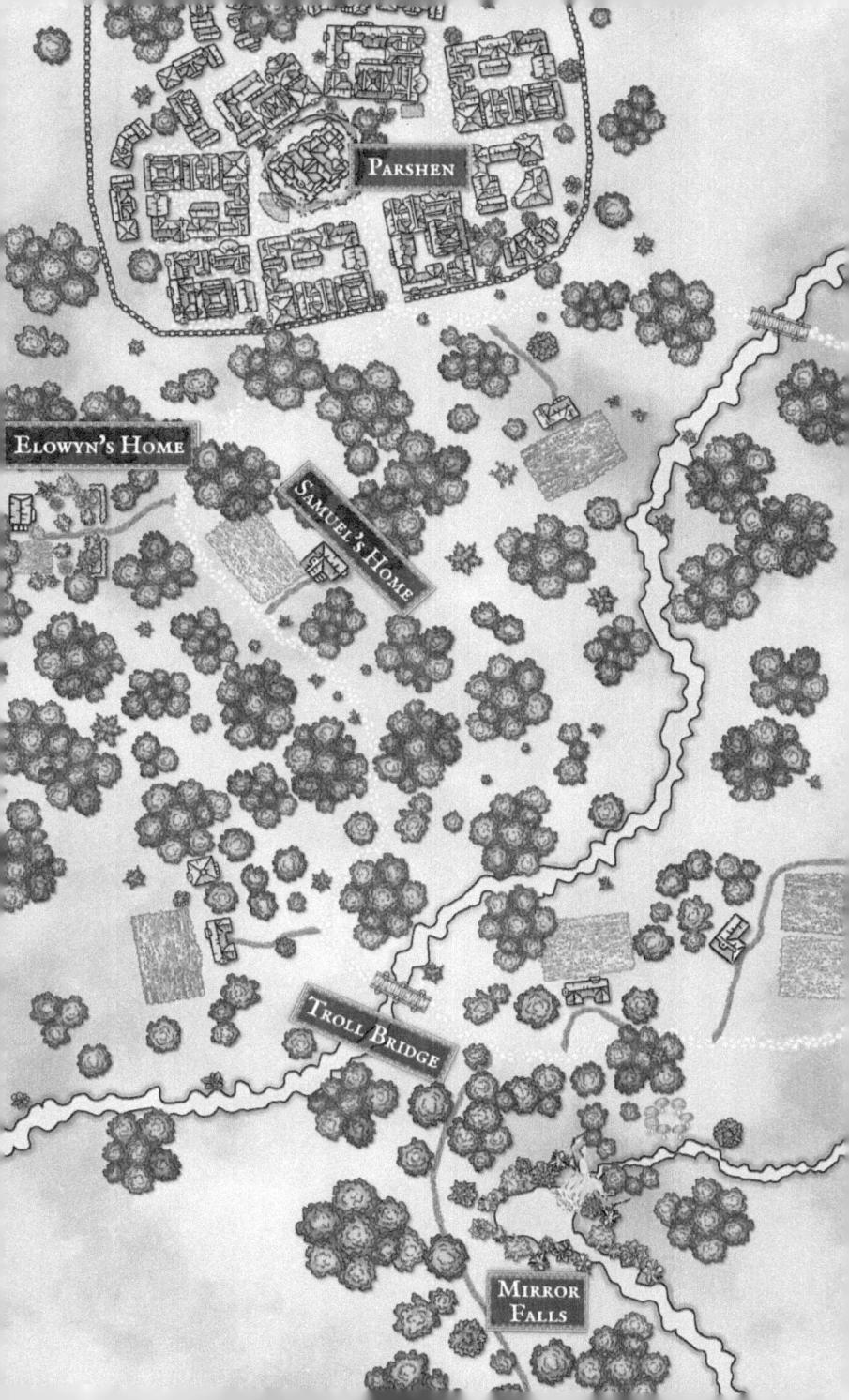

PARSHEN

ELOWYN'S HOME

SAMUEL'S HOME

TROLL BRIDGE

MIRROR FALLS

## To: All the single women in search of their frog prince

Maybe one isn't necessary?

# Chapter One

Morning doves coo overhead as I move through the early-morning streets of Parshen. Banners of royal blue and green drape the lampposts and hang from the tallest buildings. They flutter softly in the breeze, which whispers a warm promise that summer is arriving.

At this time of morning, with the sky drifting from black to watercolor clouds, the only other person I have seen is the lamplighter carrying his pole to extinguish the torches burning in the lamps. I chose this hour because I'm not likely to see many guards, if any, and I won't run into the hundreds of people who have flocked into the city. Even with a hammer and nail, I will only be a mild nuisance.

I stab my flier through the already existing nail on the post, covering up someone else's weather worn poster with nearly indistinguishable print seeking a lost pet. I'm not likely to receive a ticket for noise. Not that hanging posters would warrant a ticket, but what is *on* them might: *Protest laws forcing expensive testing and licensing of magic users. Sunset at Torgen Meadow, Thursday. King Willard forces witches and wizards from Arcoren.*

Behind me, I hear paper tear, and I bristle in anger

before turning to see who has just ripped off my flier.

A young man casually leans against the post with a half-eaten apple crumble muffin in one hand and my flier in the other. "You know you can get arrested for this, right?" he says without meeting my gaze.

The hood of his blue cloak obscures his features, but the polished pins on his green vest show he is a high rank of soldier. The buckle of his cloak is the royal shield, so he is also important enough to be near the royal family, though he isn't in the uniform of the king's guard.

"Hanging fliers isn't against the law," I point out, crossing to a horse post a few steps away and adding some distance between us. I still keep him in the corner of my vision.

He lifts his head just enough that the morning light shines on the lower half of his face and the smirk on his lips. "Holding a rally intentionally challenging the laws of the king is."

"Maybe you should take the flier to your father so I wouldn't have to hold a rally at all."

"My father?"

At this, I am unable to restrain myself and do, in fact, roll my eyes. "Your boots." I hammer a nail through the next piece of paper onto the post. I glance back at him in time to see him looking at his feet, lifting the toes of his mud-covered boots.

"What do my boots have to do with anything?"

"Sure, they're worn and dirty, but they're made of the finest leather. Not to mention the seams are in perfect shape." I give him a sickly sweet smile when he meets my gaze again. "Good morning, Prince Kaison."

He grunts, but I cannot tell if it's from amusement or annoyance. It's amazing how similarly those two emotions are emphasized in a grunt. He tugs his hood off, revealing the handsome face I haven't seen in a few months. His shoulder-length black hair is clean and groomed, though a bit messy from wearing his hood. His copper eyes dart down and back up, looking me over even though I know he's clearly been following me.

"You look good. I like your dress. It's new, isn't it?"

I turn to fully face him, holding the remainder of my fliers against my chest. It's a great alternative to my sudden desire to strangle him. He has the audacity to comment on my looks right now? "You can come to the rally if you want to. Unless you plan on shutting it down."

His lips are parted to form a response when the right corner lifts up slightly in a sort of bewildered scoffing smile. Prince Kai finally chooses to shrug off the post. "Why can't you just get your license like every other witch?"

I frown, the familiar ache in my chest quickly discarded. "We've been over this before."

"No one cares about your struggle with reading." He raises his brows in what I assume to be a gentle coaxing. "And you put together a good flier." He snaps his finger against it.

It may have been a compliment years ago, but now I can't help but feel his condescension. He lost all charm—and our friendship—a year ago when he arrested my mother and made sure she was sent to trial and imprisoned for practicing magic without a license. Not only did I lose my mother that day, but I lost my faith in the boy I'd trusted, the boy I had *almost* thought I loved. His reasons matter little to me. That kind of betrayal can never be forgotten.

Or forgiven.

I straighten my spine, but he's still almost an entire head taller than me. "To enchant and make potions, I don't need to be able to read. I'm getting along fine."

"Stubborn as ever." He shakes his head. "El, every other wizard and witch and . . . whatever else uses magic has to attend university and take an exam. Did you ever consider that if you attend a university, maybe you'd be able to learn more than just how to read? Maybe you could be more powerful."

I laugh. "You *want* me to become more powerful? Wow."

"El—"

"Stop calling me that," I interrupt. "You lost that privilege." I turn away from him and storm down the street. I've done well avoiding him every chance I've had, but he's like a dandelion that just keeps popping up out of nowhere.

He cuts in front of me. "Elowyn, I just don't want you in

prison too. That's all. This rally . . . it's your final offense."

"Are you going to arrest me too?" I glare up at him.

His lips tighten.

I don't relent.

As usual, Kai is the first to cave. His shoulders drop and he turns his face away. "I hate it when you look at me like that. I've been trying to talk to you for a long time because I wanted to explain what happened that day. You never seem to be home."

"I know." I try to step around him.

He grabs my arm, stopping me, and lowers his voice. "El, I can't help your mom or change any laws until I am king. You know this. I'm sorry for what happened. I really am. Everything I've tried . . ." He sighs and finally turns his head to meet my furious glare again. "I can't make him change. I can't convince him of anything."

I know that Kai is right. His father is the most stubborn person I've ever heard of. Though I've never met King Willard myself—other than a small run-in when we were children and I was caught slipping over the back fence into the gardens to throw a mud pie at Kai. Kai has always had very few positive things to say about his father. After all, King Willard is the entire reason I even have to hold this rally in the first place. He despises magic. But his father's attitude is no excuse for Kai betraying me. For as many times as Kai has let me go, I expected he would do the same for the only person I have left in this world. I haven't even received a letter from my mother to know how she's doing.

"I can't afford to attend university," I mutter. "So what else am I supposed to do with my time? All I have to do is to help my mother. The only way to do that is to make the king change his laws. Magic users are just as capable as anyone else of finishing an apprenticeship and proving our worth by being trained by another user of magic. Why is it good enough for every other profession to have an apprenticeship but not those who use magic?"

Kai lowers his hand to his side, takes the final bite of his muffin, then wipes his hand on his pant leg. Through the muffin, he says, "If you bring that argument to my father, do you know what he's going to do?"

I tilt my head. "Find it valid like you do?" I ask hopefully.

He swallows. "What my father would be most inclined to do is require the other occupations to take paid exams."

I frown. "Do you truly have no sway with your father?"

He blurts out a laugh and runs his fingers through his dark hair. "If you think I have any sway with my father, I wouldn't be forced to marry a princess who requires fifty mattresses to sleep." He points his thumb back toward the castle.

My heart skips.

It's his wedding day.

I was so busy remembering my anger toward him, I forgot that he's supposed to be in the castle right now, preparing to merge our kingdoms in some sort of alliance. I look him up and down.

How could I forget?

No. I didn't forget. I am in denial.

The flapping banners and influx of people into the city are all for him.

"Might feel a little pity after all?" he asks, his tone playfully sad.

I clear my throat. "First, how did you even find fifty mattresses in the city?" I step up to the side of a building and use the hammer in my hand to nail the flier into its wooden wall. "And second, how does she even climb on top?"

He holds his hands out, palms up, and shrugs. "Slugs if I know. I can't believe those are your questions right now."

"It sounds better to start off with questions like that instead of 'What is she like? Tell me all about her!' when you clearly aren't excited to be marrying her."

We stand in an uncomfortable silence until Kai breaks it. He rests a hand on his hip and gestures his other toward his body. "Look how nicely I'm dressed. What makes you think I'm not excited?"

Normal friends would be happy for one another. I should be teasing him or helping him fix his hair. He was my best friend, one of the few people in the city who would play with me in spite of my purple eye—the other being blue—and the rumors I was a witch. I'm tired of being alone after a year. But if he hadn't arrested my mother, or even spoken up in her behalf during her trial, she wouldn't be locked away for the next four years, and I wouldn't be alone in the first place.

I smile a little bit. "It's your wedding day and you're wandering the streets? Moreover, you're here. With me. Knowing how much I hate you."

Regret flashes in his eyes and his jaw hardens. "Fair enough," he mutters.

I lick my lips. I won't admit it to him, but I *do* feel bad for him. I'm not sure he had any say in this marriage. "Well, if you're looking for something to do." I hold my stack of fliers out toward the prince, completely expecting him to raise his brows—which he does. I also expect him to turn away, but he does not.

Prince Kai takes the papers from me in both hands. "Where to next?"

I stand there staring at him like a bog salamander with unblinking eyes for far too long, because why on earth is a prince agreeing to help me hang fliers deliberately holding an illegal rally to speak against his father? Even if we are—or *were*—friends, he should be doing other, far more important things right now.

"I . . . uh . . ." I finally shake myself from my stupor and gesture. "This way."

As we begin down the street, he steps up to match my pace so we are side by side. His arm brushes my shoulder, and I would be lying if I said I didn't like the sudden spark that shoots through me. I've missed his strong presence, his smile, his . . . smell.

"Have you been getting along all right? I've been worried."

The prickle of anger when he says he's worried makes my face hot. "I'm fine. I have a thriving garden, I've been able to sell things at market, and I'm still practicing magic. Don't look at me like that. I'm only practicing at home, so I'm not anywhere near the city. And I'm still doing nothing more than enchanting things, so I'm not putting anyone at risk."

"It's just . . . you know how to push the boundaries." He lowers his voice. "You shouldn't be telling me this."

I take a piece of paper from him and pin it up on the corner of a building. "You aren't going to turn me in."

Even though he arrested Mother, when I burst into her trial and his father tried to arrest me for disrupting the court, Kai stepped between us and argued that I had a right to be present. He added other technical things I can't recall, but I was allowed to stay. What I remember most is breaking down when the king sentenced Mother. Kai dragged me out before his father could change his mind and arrest me too.

We turn down an alley that leads to the main road. On a normal day, I might see a couple of people leaving their homes, heading off to jobs or to set up their carts at market.

Today is different. Many people are leaving their homes in their finest clothes. One woman holds the door open and shouts up the stairs for her partner to "Hurry so we can get a good spot!"

Kai stops just long enough to quickly pull his hood back up to hide his identity.

I reach out and take another flier. "You don't have to stay."

"I want to." He holds the flier against the post so I can hammer it in place. "How is Acorn?"

I tilt my head at the mention of my hedgehog sidekick. "Digging a hole, more than likely. Kaison, the small talk doesn't suit you. You can go if you need to. Why are you really here with me?"

He shrugs and stops in front of a bulletin board to pin one of the fliers up himself. "I suppose I was hoping you would give me a reason not to follow through with the wedding." His gaze darts to me from the corner of his eyes.

I straighten. "You . . . want me to talk you out of it?"

"Stupid, huh? I mean, who else am I going to marry? You?" He looks at me with a coy grin, one that used to send my heart into palpitations and make my stomach roll. In spite of my bitterness toward him, the familiarity of that feeling makes my heart ache.

"Oh shut up," I reply. But I used to dream about that very thing.

The bells in the castle towers ring and he turns to face

them. I hate that I can't see his full expression beyond his hood. His confession to me that he doesn't want to get married cracks the defenses I've built up against him. Knowing I am furious with him, he has still sought me out and not only spoken with me today, but more or less asked for my forgiveness. I have no doubt he would have gone all the way to my home to find me.

I'm not ready to forgive him and let him back in. But I'll always care for him.

"You're welcome to hide at my cottage, if you want," I suggest in spite of myself.

His lips tug in a sad smile and he hands me the remainder of the fliers. "Don't be surprised if I show up later." He grins, and the angle of sunlight shows his face just long enough for me to see him wink.

We both know he won't.

For a flicker of a moment, I see the young man whose bright brown eyes always saw the world with curiosity. The one who slipped me into the kitchen of the castle to steal an orange because I had never tasted one. The one who showed me how to hold a sword and attempted to teach me how to fight with it. The boy who snuck me a basket of food on my birthday two months ago when I refused to open the door for him.

"Good day, Lady Elowyn." He bows to me, a formal gesture he rarely uses with me.

"I'm not a lady," I protest as he begins to turn away.

His gaze lingers. "You are to me."

I suck my lips into my mouth and my anger dissipates with every step away from me he takes.

I should yell at him to come back.

I can't imagine being forced into a marriage I don't want. Kaison was my dearest friend my entire life. Was. I wish so many things in this kingdom could change. Maybe it really will be best for Kaison to marry a proper princess in order to take the throne and make the changes the people need. Maybe then I can forgive him.

But what will he need of my forgiveness if he's married to someone else?

## Chapter Two

"You've hardly said a word since Prince Brown Eyes left."

I look over at Acorn, the hedgehog who has adopted me as his family since I rescued him from a hawk three years ago. He sits on a bundle of green fabric he has wedged between bottles of dried ingredients I've accumulated from plant roots, petals, and stems. The wing of a moth hangs out of his mouth as he finishes consuming it.

After hanging my fliers, I retreated to my wagon I've covered into a mobile shop. I've set up my wagon on the edge of the market square, beside one of the few grass patches where my trusty donkey can nibble while I work.

"How did you know I saw him? You weren't with me."

He tilts his head. "You smell like him. And now you're sad, and you're only this kind of sad when you see him."

"I'm distracted by everything I have to prepare for today and then the rally." I reach up above the counter to a shelf I've added to my wagon.

"You only get quiet when you're thinking. Or sad." Acorn's little nails clatter across the countertop to reach me.

"There's just a lot to do." I crouch to get everything off of the shelves to set out on display so when the time comes,

I can pull up the fabric on the side of the wagon and sell right out of here instead of setting up tables.

"You got all of your fliers hung?"

"Almost all of them. I would have liked to add more out on Canal Street, but there were just too many people and . . ." I sigh.

To be honest, I wasn't so excited about the rally anymore once people flooded the streets, vibrating in excitement for the royal wedding. And I couldn't get Kai's words out of my head that he couldn't do anything to change laws or help my mother until he is king. Does that mean he is marrying this princess just to become king?

The first basket I set out is a basket of painted rocks. The children in town love the colorful dots I paint on whatever flat stones I can find, and they line up with handfuls of coins, in spite of their parents' fears I'm an evil bog witch. My single purple eye doesn't help with this fear.

Acorn twitches his nose. "Just think. In a few days, you might have some people to sign your petition. Considering how much you talk about this, I'm betting you'll get . . . oh . . . twenty signatures? Do you think that will be sufficient for the king to rewrite the law?" I don't miss the sarcasm in his tone.

I lean on the counter and place a fist on my hip. "You're such an optimist."

"I'm sure the whole event is going to go well." He nods. "How many soldiers do you think he'll send to stop you?"

I scowl down at the hedgehog. "Rallies aren't illegal. People hold them all the time." I refocus my attention on my wares.

"Yes, well, they don't have a king who outright dislikes them either." He has a point, but it's moot. "You're lucky he doesn't arrest you outright for merely selling enchanted things."

I have to be careful not to outright advertise enchanted items. I frequently have young ladies ask for a necklace to help them catch the gaze of a suitor. While I *could* perform an enchantment to help someone fall in love, I personally feel that is cheating and people should fall in love because they want to. So I usually put some sort of sparkle charm to make them stand out a bit more, but they have to rely on their own personality from there.

A farmer once asked for an enchanted log to keep away pests, which was so successful I got a line of farmers begging for their own. That one is what got me my second fine. One more fine means jail time, and I'm not ready to risk that yet.

Acorn tilts his head at me as he leans it over the edge of the counter. "It sounded to me like he wants you to help him escape his wedding. *That* would give them a reason to arrest you."

I adjust the basket of rocks to keep my hands busy. "Acorn, you know how I feel about him. Considering how much you love our life, I'm shocked you *want* me to help him. If I get arrested, what becomes of you?"

"What's stopping you from just snatching him and marrying him instead?"

"Acorn! Enough! I won't forgive him! Besides that, Kai is a prince. I'm a witch on the brink of getting arrested just for existing."

He squeaks. "That's true. I mean." He turns in a circle. "You forgot to mention you're poor."

"Thanks for pointing that out too," I mutter. "At least I'm surviving."

"Yep." His head bounces up and down. "Selling tonic water to help bald men, or a bundle of sage for someone completely inexperienced to banish what they think is a ghost haunting their barn." He waddles his spiky body over to a basket of polished rocks and grips the straw edge with his little fingers. "And you've even resorted to selling rocks."

"Those aren't just rocks. These rocks are *enchanted*." I point out the runes I've carved into them. They aren't pretty.

"Ah. Of course they are," Acorn replies sarcastically and slowly nods his head in a pathetic attempt to show honesty. Though I'm not sure he's actually trying to hide his attitude. He's never been good at that, and he's on one today.

I hold up a rock with a three-ring swirl with a line through it. "This symbol means good fortune."

"Are you certain?" he asks. "Because I believe that may be the cursed symbol for drought."

In a moment of doubt, I pull out my mother's grimoire from my pouch—I'm never without it—and flip to the torn page signifying the beginning of the section on charms. I flip two pages, set the green leather-bound book down, and point so the pessimistic rodent can see it. (Don't ever tell him I called him a rodent. He insists he isn't.) "I can read well enough to know this means good fortune."

"Well, it looks an awful lot like the curse," Acorn counters, not offering an apology. He falls back down on all fours. "I hardly call this a good use of your magic, and it is a pathetic way to make money. Can you really enchant a rock?"

I shift from one foot to the other, close the book, and fumble to shove it back into my pouch. "Well, yes."

"But?"

"Admittedly, the enchantment, once summoned, only lasts a short period of time." I place my hands on my hips.

"Why?"

"Regular stone has little earth-granted energy and barely holds on to any enchantment or curse. I should use crystals or other energy-driven materials, but I haven't had the time to find them. Today is the prince's wedding and the crowds will be out in full." I lean one hand on the counter. "People who buy don't need to know they won't last."

"You? Lying?" He reaches out and puts his tiny hand on mine. I swear he's smirking. "I'm proud of how much you've grown."

"I have to live somehow." I turn away from him to assure all has been set up. "It makes them keep coming back. That's good business, wouldn't you agree?" I'm not sure Mother would be proud of me. She had built her reputation on kindness, honesty, and generosity. But I'm trying to survive, and right now, the lines of honesty can do with a little blurring so I have money for what I cannot make.

"I think you should go to the wedding."

I blink as I face him. "What?"

"No one is going to be here for hours." His nose twitches. "If you don't take me, I'll go watch myself."

I roll my eyes, imagining a tiny hedgehog trying to make his way to the castle. Knowing him, he would find some way to disrupt the festivities by getting under someone's feet, eating the bouquet, or some other thing to initiate the kind of adventure he constantly talks about.

"Fine," I mutter. "I'll take you. But I don't know that I'll stay the whole time. We leave when I'm ready."

"Agreed!" he squeaks with excitement.

Picking him up, I climb out the back of the wagon.

Have I mentioned how much I despise crowds? It looks like the entire kingdom of Arcoren has shown up for Prince Kai's wedding, and they crowd the streets so tightly I can barely move. I keep to the edge as much as possible until I work my way to a tree near the gates away from a majority of the crowd pushing to look through the front gates. A cluster of boys sit in the boughs.

One beams down at me. He's missing his top two front

teeth and has just lost one of his bottom—he told me yesterday when he bought a red painted rock. "Ellie! There's room for you too!"

"Can you climb up?" another asks.

"Of course I can," I state. "I'm a tree-climbing expert." I hesitate only because I'm wearing my new dress, the only one I own without a hole. It's a beautiful, deep shade of lavender and matches my slightly pointed purple hat.

I pull the back of my skirt between my legs for some level of modesty and tuck it into my belt before I grab the lowest branch with my hands, plant my foot on a ridge in the trunk, and pull myself up. I shift so I'm sitting on the thickest part of the branch nearest the trunk, careful not to tear my dress.

"This is definitely a much better view," I say.

"Yeah! We can see over the wall!" He points, completely oblivious to the guard in the archer's tower to his right.

I manage to make eye contact with that soldier and he pats his crossbow. I nod at him, acknowledging the warning.

I stretch up a bit higher to see over the wall a bit better. We have a clear view of the mighty castle doors, but there isn't a crowd, priest, or guest anywhere to be seen outside, only the soldiers standing all across the grounds, watching for anyone who may be a threat.

I recall Kai's expression as he walked with me that very morning. I was so focused on my own anger toward him, I didn't pay much attention to his tight smile and darting eyes. He had been afraid. He didn't want to get married. He had come to see me and I had pushed him away. Rightfully so, of course, but . . .

Now he is somewhere within the walls of the castle, holding hands with a princess he doesn't know, preparing to vow a life of allegiance to a complete stranger and her kingdom.

For what?

I don't know whether his loyalty to the throne is his fatal flaw or redeeming quality.

The castle bells jar me from my thoughts so suddenly, I'm grateful I have a grip on the tree, or I would have fallen.

"We present to you Prince Kaison and his betrothed, Princess Genoa!"

Acorn wiggles in the pouch and his voice is muted. "Are you going to let me see him?"

Reluctantly, I reach in and lift him out.

The front doors open and a woman in a glittering gold dress steps into the sunlight. The top of the gown fits every perfect curve and is lavishly adorned with gold and silver beads, and pearls. It flares out just above her knee, where there is a slit to show off her pure-white heels and irritatingly perfect legs. She's literally sparkling in the late morning sun.

Her face?

Well, even that is perfect. Her skin seems to glow and she has a narrow chin, tiny little nose, and bright blue eyes.

She's the most beautiful person I've ever seen. Her blonde hair is braided into two braids coming up the back of her head until they reach her ears, where the braids drape back down behind them. Her long, pointed ears.

My brows pinch.

A fairy?

Kai is marrying a literal fairy?

She wears a headpiece that dangles a ruby pendant onto her forehead. Her smile is just as radiant as everything else, and she waves perfectly manicured fingers at the screaming crowd. Her wings are a dull orange.

My attention shifts to Kai.

Prince Kaison.

Soon to be king, I suppose.

I suddenly don't feel so bad for Kai anymore. He didn't tell me she was a fairy. Maybe there's a reason he kept it all secret. The kingdom hasn't exactly been on good terms with them for decades. Perhaps this marriage isn't about him becoming king so much as securing some kind of alliance with the banished race.

Kai wears a white uniform with a gold vest, which is adorned with all of his military pins. He wears no cloak, and his boots are new and nearly reach his knees. The high collar of the shirt almost touches his clean-shaven jaw. He is the ideal complement to his bride. His raven hair has been trimmed to below his ears and oiled back. He looks like everything a prince and king should be.

But he doesn't look like the Kai I know.

The Kai I know has muddy boots and dirt under his nails, his messy long hair tied back, and a loud laugh. He's not even smiling the way Kai smiles. His lips are too tight and the muscles in his jaw are clenched.

My heart suddenly aches.

I should have tried harder to talk with him about how I feel. How I felt he had abandoned me when I needed him the most. Maybe we could have worked through all of this. Maybe he wouldn't be here beside a stranger.

Who am I kidding? As Acorn mentioned earlier, I am not suited to marry a prince. I'm the bog witch, living in a cottage stuffed with plants, selling pathetically charmed or enchanted items to have just enough money to buy bread. This princess has an entire kingdom to give Kai, armies to add to ours, and incredible beauty. She will give him what he needs. The things I could never provide.

I know better.

He's a prince. I am *not* a princess.

I live in a cottage in the woods with a leak in the window.

He lives in a castle in the center of Parshen.

Kai's copper eyes somehow meet mine. I don't know how in the five winds he managed to see me up here in the tree when there is a throng of people waving at him. I suppose that it's because this isn't the first time he has found me in this tree and he was hoping I would be here.

I want to yell at him that there is still time to escape, but I try and smile instead.

The corner of his lip lifts ever so slightly and he tilts his chin to me. Acknowledgement that he feels the same hollow feeling building in my chest? A final apology? Goodbye?

A stupid gust of wind blows a stupid particle of sand into my eyes and tears immediately fill them. I drop down from the tree before Kai can mistake my tears for feelings toward him. I have to get back to my wagon and open it for when the crowd begins the day of celebration. And I can't bear to sit up in that tree while Kai returns to the castle to officially marry the woman at his side.

If it weren't for Acorn, I would have no one.

When I get back to my mobile shop, I swallow the lump in my throat, grab the rope, and pull it to roll back the fabric on the side of the wagon to expose my wares. What I need right now is distraction.

Feelings are so overrated.

## Chapter Three

My cheeks ache from smiling all day and I simply cannot wait to get home, sit in my armchair by the fire, and sip some warm ginger tea with a couple of drops of my inflammation tonic. Even though the sun's light is extending, I don't begin cleaning up my wagon until the sun has long since set. The celebration that has been in the streets all night is finally done, save a cluster of drunken men singing a street or two over.

I drop the fabric on the wagon to cover the open side and tie it down. With that done and my interior secure, I walk around to collect my donkey from where I tied him this morning.

Pancho grazes at the fence on the edge of a potato farm.

"Did you have a good day being spoiled by the children?" I ask, noticing the flower braided on top of his head with the expertise of a child.

He tilts his head, lifts his lip, and lets out a loud laugh.

I cannot resist a smile.

"A little girl brought me an apple," Pancho boasts.

"What a lovely treat." I rub the length of his gray nose. "Ready to go home?"

"Oh yes. I need sleep." He bounces his head up and down.

"Are you getting old?" I tease, giving him scritches behind his tall ears.

"Me? Are you? Do you not sleep?"

I laugh. It feels good to laugh after such a long and busy day. "Oh, Pancho." I hug him around the neck and give him a kiss on his cheek. "Let's go home."

Pancho drags the rickety old wagon down the road, the only sound at this time of night the grinding of our wheels on the stones and dirt, and an owl hooting from a tree. The frogs have long since gone to bed, as have the crickets.

Acorn crawls out from the pouch he sleeps in during the day and sits on my lap to nibble on some nuts he either found or had stored, and I absently stroke his spikes while I watch the stars.

Kai's ceremony happened hours ago, before lunch. They probably had a huge table—or multiple—with food enough to feed all of their royal guests. I wonder how many royal friends dined with him. Did he laugh at their jokes? Did he dance for hours with his new wife? Do his feet hurt? He used to laugh as he taught me to dance and always told me I was better than him.

Is he now in his honeymoon suite?

I run my hands down my face and pull the hat from my head. I should be focusing on what to pull together for market tomorrow. With the celebration over, visitors should be leaving and will want last-minute shopping before they go.

Somewhere in my braid my hair is tight and causing a headache, so I untie my braid and tug it loose, rubbing my scalp with my fingers.

I'm lost in the haze of exhaustion and comfort of the familiar journey when I hear someone yell, "Wait!"

I blink myself awake, unsure if I heard correctly, because it's practically the middle of the night and no one should be awake right now.

"Hold on!" The voice is small, like Acorn's, so it's either a small child or an animal.

"Pancho, stop." I set Acorn on the bench before sliding to the ground and crouching to search the shadows. "Hello?"

A very ordinary bullfrog hops toward me as fast as possible. Why is it out on the road at this time of night?

"Is it you calling for me?"

"Yes. You. I need help. I've been turned into a frog!" He sounds out of breath.

I reach out with a little smile. "If you're a human, what is your name?"

He swallows, pulling his eyes in for a blink. "Kai. Prince Kaison."

My smile drops and I study the frog over.

I have spoken with animals since I was a child, but I've never had an animal claim to have been turned into one.

"A frog prince?" I finally ask. "If you need a sanctuary, you—"

"It's me, Elowyn! I was with Genoa and she handed me a gold ball, and the next thing I knew . . . well, look at me!" A part of me genuinely cannot believe that *Prince* Kai is sitting before me in the form of a frog. I am inclined not to believe him until he lets out a frustrated croak. "El. I came and walked with you this morning and helped you hang your fliers. I need your help now!"

No frog would have known Kai helped me this morning.

I reach out and pick up his cold little body and lift him for a better look. The only thing that looks remotely like the man I know are his golden eyes. "If you really are Kai—"

"I am!"

An overwhelming rush of confusion, worry, and disbelief rushes over me like a wave. If this is Kai . . .

"Then it's a curse or enchantment," I mutter. "Which means whatever you touched has an enchantment or curse on it, otherwise it wouldn't have turned you. Do you have it?"

"Let me pull it out of my pocket," he replies sarcastically.

"Right." I shake my head.

"I hopped out of the window as soon as I realized I'm not me anymore. I didn't know where else to go but to you, especially since your expertise is enchantments. You must know a way to break it."

I stand and return to the wagon, holding Kai in my hands. This can't be real. A frog version of Kai. I look down at him as I take my seat.

He croaks. "I know you're shocked. So am I. Tell me what to do."

"I don't know, to be honest." I shake my head and set him on my lap. "I'm still wrapping my head around you being a frog. Pancho, head home."

The donkey doesn't hesitate to resume his leisurely pace.

"I can't analyze the spell on you without the item it came from." I massage my eyebrow. "Gold is a powerful conductor for magic, so whoever created it knew what they were doing. Do you think your princess did it intentionally?"

He shakes his head. "I don't know. It seemed innocent enough." He blinks deeply. "I don't know, El. I'm confused. After it happened, I felt so strange and I panicked, and all I wanted to do was find you."

I dig into my pouch to fish out my mother's grimoire. "I've never created a transfiguration enchantment, but maybe Mother has."

The grimoire is mother's journal of magical spells, enchantments, and documentation she has collected since she began learning magic. Like my own grimoire, hers has some spells from other witches too. But it's too dark to read. I search my pocket to produce a black, lightweight stone filled with hundreds of holes. It's a piece of lava stone Mother traded for, and the first thing I enchanted. With the natural properties from the earth, I was able to enchant it as a stone of light. All I have to do is whisper *"luminair."* The glow offers just enough light for me to flip through the pages and read. At one point the pages were alphabetical, but now there is so much information there is barely room for new entries.

"Enchantments are usually temporary, so we could wait to see what happens. Of course, if it's a curse then it could get worse," I mutter.

The rest of the journey home I flip through the pages, searching for anything that has to do with shape-shifting or transfiguration or anything else.

"We're home," Pancho whinnies.

"He talked!" frog version of Kai states.

"You can understand him?" I ask.

"Yes! Wait . . . you've always been able to talk to animals. This is what it's like?"

Acorn leans forward from around my side to take a look at the frog. "Is he always this dim?"

"Acorn," I say with a sigh. "Be nice. He's never heard animals speak before."

Kai's eyes seem wide, but at the same time, bullfrogs just have open eyes, so I can't tell if he's as shocked as his silence indicates.

I climb down, taking Kai in one hand and Acorn in the

other, then set Acorn on the top step in front of the door. "Scamper in and get one of the candles lit while I take care of Pancho."

"Yes, madam!" He scuttles away.

I set Kai on Pancho's back. "Why wouldn't you go to the royal sorcerer? Or the university? Especially since you value their education." I was being intentionally snarky to see how the frog would react.

He doesn't immediately answer, but then says, "Because I trust you?"

I frown. "You do?"

His sides puff out and his throat swells before he sighs. "Why does that surprise you so much?"

"Considering how I've . . . been toward you lately. I haven't—"

"Did I not come see you this morning?"

"Well, yes." I shift my weight.

"You're my friend."

"Such a good friend."

"Maybe I should go back to the castle," Kai mutters.

My chest tightens. For someone who missed him and felt bad minutes ago, I'm doing a fantastic job letting him know. "It's dangerous this time of day. We have a hawk that hunts the meadow."

Kai says nothing more while I take care of Pancho. I add some fresh water to his basin, check his salt block, and drop fresh straw into the paddock before I grab Kai and close the gate behind me.

The tense silence between us makes my heart ache. Today is the most we've been near one another in a year, and I'm making it miserable for us both. What makes it so hard to talk to him?

When I enter my home, Acorn has lit the candle beside the sink to offer enough light I can make out the shapes of my home and not bruise my chin again on the chest by the door. He scurries around to collect ingredients for what I assume to be dinner.

I set Kai on the countertop and clap my hands. "*Luminair*!" All of the candles, lanterns, and even fireplace light.

My family cottage is everything I could want in a home. The sink is positioned in the corner of the kitchen, where the windows have a curved alcove, which makes it convenient to have the most sun-desperate plants year-round. That window overlooks the frog pond, little barn, and meadow.

To the right is the fireplace, made of beautiful dark stones, which currently has bundles of plants dangling down to dry. On the wall to the right of that is the work bench my mother and I have carefully made over the years. There are shelves hanging the entire length of the wall, packed with jars containing every important ingredient I have collected, all organized in alphabetical order. Bark shavings, sap, roots, leaves, stems, ash, oils, water (different types of water hold different properties like every other living thing), bones, bone powder, sand, and so much more.

The counter in front of the shelves is more organized chaos, with smaller jars and bottles for tonics or poultices, bowls for mixing, mortar and pestle, enchanted crystals, and other such important items. While I have my mother's grimoire in my pouch, my personal grimoire sits open on the counter. With Mother being gone, I've been working on a few of my own ideas. Mother's strength is in healing with nature, so I've kept that close to my heart.

Glancing at Kai, I can't help but feel a part of me longing for the further knowledge of enchantment. If I knew more, I'd be able to help him. As much as I hate to admit it, Kai is right. I can't just *read* how to enchant. I need to be taught. And the only way for that to happen is if I find another witch willing to teach me or attend the university. Mother is no longer here to help. But going to university won't work for someone like me, not when letters jump around the page as I try to read them as if they've made a game of me failing to catch hold of their meaning.

I busy myself in the kitchen by setting a pot with water on the rack over the fire into which I sprinkle some salt, then I turn to grab some small yellow potatoes. I pause and glance at Kai. "I imagine you won't be able to eat human food like this. You must be hungry."

He croaks in response.

I purse my lips and look at Acorn.

He pouts immediately, pinching his brows forward so his spikes almost cover his eyes entirely. "I don't want to share my worms!" He scuttles over to the little jar beneath the window where we store his worms.

"He only needs a few, and we can look for more when he's back to being human. Just enough for dinner and breakfast." I lean on the counter. "I noticed some plump caterpillars on the apple tree yesterday. We can go get some of them too."

Acorn huffs. "Promise?"

"Promise."

"Fine," he grumbles.

I take the container and pull out a worm, then set it on the counter a little bit away from Kai. "There you go."

Kai looks at it, then up at me and back. "How am I supposed to eat that? It's a worm!"

I shrug and resume washing the potatoes. "You're a frog now. Use your tongue?"

"I wasn't asking about logistics." He groans out a loud croak. "This is going to be disgusting." He hops forward, clamping his mouth around the worm, and desperately flicks his head to force the worm into his mouth and down his throat. His eyes suck into his head as he swallows.

"Well?" I ask, dropping my diced potatoes into the water to boil. "How does it taste?"

"Like dirt," he mutters. "But also a little bit gamy like . . . lamb."

"Lamb? Hm." I lean over, untie my shoes, and pull them off. "That's better." I rub the big toe on my left foot. I desperately need a slightly bigger pair of shoes, but that will have to wait until I have enough money. Maybe I should have gotten shoes instead of the dress. "So explain to me again why you didn't just run to the royal sorcerer?"

Kai hops closer. "We don't have one. Father fired him months ago."

I raise both of my eyebrows. "I suppose that shouldn't surprise me, but it does." I tug out the stems and scrub some portobello mushrooms.

He grunts—or croaks.

"Then why did you run away from your bride?"

"I panicked." He stops at the edge of the counter.

"Why?"

"We finished the marriage celebration and were in the bridal suite. I had just started talking to her about sleeping arrangements, but she cut me off saying she had a wedding gift made just for me. When I opened the box, there was a golden ball inside. It didn't seem significant and I picked it up. It felt like I got struck by lightning. I couldn't breathe, and it actually hurt my entire body. When I could see again, everything was enormous and I was a frog."

I dry my hands on a towel. "Being tricked by a fairy surprises you?"

Kai blinks at me. "A what?"

"Fairy. I mean, if marrying one was your plan all along,

you could have just told me. You didn't need to keep that secret." I start mixing the ingredients together to stuff into the mushrooms.

"El, what are you talking about? She's just a princess."

I stop to look at him. "You couldn't see her wings?"

Kai's frog face scrunches. "Wings?"

"She has pointed ears too."

When he doesn't respond, I draw the conclusion that Kai must not have seen because of some kind of glamour. I have heard fairies can disguise themselves as humans to lure human victims, but as far as I know, fairies have been locked away in their realm for as long as I've been alive.

He shakes his head. "All I know is that after I touched the orb, she didn't seem surprised I was a frog. She only reacted when I started hopping away and tried chasing me down."

"Do you think she intentionally did it?" I wonder.

He heaves a sigh. "I don't know. My head hurts."

"Why do you think she would make you a frog?" I shove the last of the mixture into the last mushroom and set it in the pan beside the others.

Kai lowers his body against the counter, making his belly squish out. "I'm too tired to know. I thought about it the whole time hopping to you, but the only idea that keeps coming to mind is motivation to take the throne. I barely know her."

"I think we should take you to your father first thing

tomorrow."

"Uh I wouldn't do that."

"Why not?"

"Think about it. This morning you hung fliers advertising a rally against my father, I've been missing all night, and then you show up at the castle with me as a frog in your hands?"

Realization dawns on me and I lean my back against the counter. "Your father will think I turned you into a frog as some sort of leverage?"

"Exactly." He nods.

I massage my temples. My night has become far more complicated than it should be. "Okay. Then the only thing I can think of is to sneak me into the castle so I can get that orb. There has to be residual magic, and I may be able to figure out the spell. If I can reveal the enchantment or curse, we can figure out how to fix things from there."

I hear his body plop against the counter as he moves closer. "Elowyn?"

"Hm?" I drop my hands and turn my head to look at him.

"Thanks." I can't tell if he's trying to smile. Frog faces don't move the same way human faces do, but I think that's what he's going for. "I really didn't know where else to go."

I smile back. "I'm glad you thought of me."

"I guess I ended up sneaking off to you anyway."

"This is not exactly how I imagined you showing up."

"I am technically naked," he teases.

"Kai." I press my hand to my forehead.

Kai chuckles, but it sounds more like a croak. "Don't worry. We'll figure this out. How complicated can it be?"

## Chapter Four

The fog of morning dreams dissipates from my mind as I sip my cup of hot tea from the armchair by the fireplace and stare at the frog soaking in a shallow dish of water on the counter. I did not dream Kai was a frog prince. The frog *is* Kai, and he has, indeed, been cursed.

Nowhere in my mother's grimoire does it mention a counter curse.

Acorn smacks his lips and curls up into a ball on my pillow, letting out a little purr like he normally does when falling asleep.

"What's the plan?" Kai asks.

I shake my head, take another sip of tea, and set the cup down on the corner of the island. "We need to get the ball and take it to the royal sorcerer your father fired. Or to the university library so I can do some research into breaking you from this spell." I cross the room to the wardrobe and pull out the purple dress I had on yesterday. "Turn away, I'm getting dressed." I glance over to watch him turn his body so he's facing out the window.

I really hope there's some god or goddess or magical godmother who can give me an idea how to save him, because I need some divine intervention.

I've only just replaced my nightgown with my underdress when Kai says, "Elowyn, soldiers are coming."

"What?" I scramble to pull my dress on, but I haven't tied the front bodice before there is a knock so loud it rattles the frame. "One moment!" I call. My hands start to shake as I tie the knot. I can't get it to tie.

There's another knock. "Open up!"

I unlock the door before opening it. "I said one moment," I reply firmly. "I was getting dressed."

A man with broad shoulders, wavy chestnut hair, and cold blue eyes stands on my porch. "We need you to come with us." He appears to be around the same age as Kai, or possibly a little older. I can't really tell because of his facial hair. He has stubble on his jaw, but a rather unflattering mustache, so wide it curls at the tips, rests beneath his nose. I've always hated mustaches.

Three more soldiers stand behind him. Wait. They have the same pin on their cloaks as Kai wore yesterday, marking them as palace guards, but their cloaks aren't blue. They're gold with blue embroidery, meaning they are the king's guard.

My stomach knots.

"I . . ." I swallow the lump growing in my throat. "I haven't received a fine or summons." I try to offer a smile, but my heart is pounding.

The man withdraws a parchment from somewhere and

flicks it in the air as he sticks it out toward me. "Consider this your summons. Let's go." He tries to grab my arm.

I jerk free. "First of all, you never grab a woman like that. Especially when I'm not under arrest. Second, you need to give me time to read."

He folds his arms, lips tight. Clearly, he doesn't want to be here any more than I want him here.

I open the parchment. There is an official seal at the bottom and a very short note which only reads: *Elowyn Grace Rotish, you are here . . . b . . . here . . . by . . . hereby?* What a strange word. *Hereby summoned to the castle.* The letter offers no explanation as to why, though there are two I can choose from: 1) the rally—unlikely given the current circumstances, and 2) well, the current circumstances.

When I lift my gaze, I realize the three men behind the mustache man have their hands on their weapons. They must have been given orders to force me should I refuse to come willingly.

Clearly, I have no choice.

I clear my throat and glance sideways at Kai. I should make him hide. "Give me one moment. I need my shoes and a few things."

Whiskers puts his hand on the door forcefully, though I've made no movement to close it.

"Relax," I mutter. I go to where I left my boots the night before, which conveniently places me near Kai. He has climbed out of the dish and left water blobs on the counter behind him. "Do you want to come?" I whisper as I tug on my first boot.

"Absolutely. You aren't leaving me."

I scoop him up and collect my shoulder bag in the same movement. It allows me to slip Kai into my dress pocket so I can put Acorn in my pouch.

"What else do you need?" Whiskers barks.

"My hedgehog. There's a stray cat by the barn who keeps trying to get him." I pick him up and show him to the man, who appears entirely unamused. "You're such a delight," I say sarcastically and put Acorn away.

The last thing I take is my wide-brimmed purple hat. "Lead the way, I guess."

The leader turns sharply, but the others wait until I pass them before they pick up the rear, leading me to a waiting wagon with an open top.

Panic strips my throat of moisture and I desperately try to swallow. Is this what Mother felt like when Kai arrested her? I look back at my home and can't imagine leaving my daughter behind. I swallow hard.

The journey into Parshen feels longer than usual, and I constantly have to remind myself to breathe through the cold rush of fear that ebbs and flows like a wave.

The castle rests at the top of the only hill for miles, and the city spreads out beneath. The road travels up it in a slow incline that curves with the hill in almost a complete circle before reaching the front gates. When I step out of the wagon, I take a moment to really take in the beauty. As a child, I never entered through the front doors. The castle is stunning, with thousands of stones piled carefully atop one another. One wide, square tower juts up in the center with smaller circular towers jammed up against its sides and a low, wide building in front. The stones are covered with vibrant green and yellow moss, and deep-brown slates adorn the roofs.

I've never noticed the colors of the windows from so far, but they are tall and each has a beautifully crafted section of stained glass at the top in the pattern of trees, vines, or flowers. A vine of morning glory has entombed the north corner of the castle and stretches its tendrils through the grooves of the stone, preparing to take over the entire northern face.

The brass hinges of the arched oak door groan with effort as the soldiers push it open to allow me to enter. I don't have time to take in much of the detail of the interior, only that it is one massive open space to the right and a grand staircase at the back, with two soldiers standing guard on either side of the double doors at the top. I wonder if the large flower arrangements standing everywhere are left over from the wedding the day prior.

I am guided into the throne room to my left. The king— wearing deep royal blue with gold and green accents—paces in front of his throne. His wife sits with what appears to be a war metal in her hand, her eyes vacant and distant. The woman I saw yesterday, Kai's wife, kneels at the queen's side, holding her hands. Genoa still has wings and pointed ears, and I have half a thought to take Kai out of my pouch and show him how Genoa is in fact a fairy, but I decide against it when all three turn to face me.

"You seem suddenly nervous," the mustached guard states flatly. He's standing directly behind my right shoulder, and his unexpected statement makes me jump.

I scowl up at him. "*Suddenly*? You're clearly not observant. I've been nervous the entire way here."

His eyes slowly move to look down at me. "Is it because you feel guilty?"

"Guilty of what?"

King Willard's face contorts in anger. "You. What did you do with my son?" He stalks over to me.

I step back, fear taking control. "Your son?" I blurt. I know what he means, but I'm too scared to say anything else.

The blonde-haired fairy climbs to her feet. "This morning, I woke to find my precious new husband trapped in the body of a frog!" Her makeup is as perfect as it was yesterday, and there isn't a wrinkle on her gown.

I feel my eyes pinch. This morning? Kai was definitely a frog yesterday. Why lie about the time? "How do you know he is a frog and not just out on a walk?" I don't mean to sound condescending. Or do I? Because I don't like her, and if she really *did* turn Kai into a frog, I have a good reason.

She scoffs and looks down her nose at me. She evidently doesn't like me either. "I know what a frog looks like. He was a human, touched something, and became a frog. Tell me that isn't an enchantment."

My brows dip. How could she know he touched something if she had just woken up? I shift my attention to the king and place a hand on my chest to play with the strap of my shoulder pouch. "I'm sorry, but why am *I* here?"

"I had you brought here to explain yourself," he says flatly. Okay, so he *does* believe I am the one who did it.

I burst out in laughter, because my frozen mind thinks that's the best reaction in this situation, and I force myself to stop. I clear my throat. "I'm sorry. I don't have that kind of magic. My expertise is in enchantments and medical remedies. Not transforming people."

"Which is why you are guilty." He says *guilty* so sharply it echoes in my mind. He used the same tone when sentencing my mother. King Willard stands over me, his intimidating presence threatening to squash me. "You have always been a thorn in my side. You've been a terrible influence on Kaison his entire life! He was turned when he touched the golden orb. An *enchanted* orb." The king snaps his fingers loudly and points to me. "Show her!" He wheels and I flinch, anticipating a blow that doesn't come. He storms over to his throne and sits.

Golden orb?

I don't know why it's taken me so long to connect the

dots between a golden orb and Princess Genoa being a fairy, but there has been a legend of a golden orb tied to fairy folklore for as long as I know. Which makes me believe not only did Genoa know Kai would be turned into a frog, but that she planned the entire event.

"We . . . couldn't find it," a servant standing at the edge of the room answers. I hadn't even noticed him.

"Perhaps Princess Genoa can assist you in finding it?" he says through gritted teeth.

Genoa appeared startled that he would recommend she help, and her eyes narrowed. "I will not get on my knees to search. It disappeared. I don't know where it went!"

"Then bring forth the prince!" The king snaps his fingers.

A young woman steps forward, carrying a pillow with a frog resting on top of it. When the servant stops in front of me, I note the poor amphibian's throat quickly moving in nervous breaths.

"You must be terrified," I say gently.

It bellows out a low croak, and I'm the only one in the room who hears a single word in that croak: "Home!"

I shake my head. "They're going to be very disappointed."

"Why would we be disappointed?" the king interjects.

"Careful," Kai whispers.

I straighten my spine and round my shoulders. "Because this frog is an ordinary pond frog. It isn't Prince

Kai . . . son."

King Willard's eyes widen. "How do you know this?"

I feel my pocket shift and slip my hand into it to push Kai back down. It's not the right time to reveal he is with me. I understand Kai may want to tell him, and that he hopefully wants to protect me from his father's wrath, but I cannot help but feel that showing Kai right now will only confirm his father's accusations. Besides that, if Princess Genoa is actually the one responsible, we don't know the reason why, and I'm not about to let Kai be snatched up now. She's acting innocent, but her calculating eyes and tight lips tell another story.

"I can . . ." I draw a breath, reluctant to admit this as it seems too convenient, but what else can I say? "I can speak with animals. This is just an ordinary frog, likely from the castle pond, who possibly slipped inside for a bit of warmth and couldn't find its way out. It's nothing but an ordinary frog."

The king scoffs. "If you can speak with animals, would you tell me if it really were Prince Kaison?"

"Why would I lie?" I shoot back. "He is my friend and I don't want anything to happen to him."

King Willard's jaw grinds and he leans back against his throne. For just a moment, the blink of an eye, his cold exterior falters just long enough for me to see his desperation. But I don't feel any pity for him. "Why should I believe you?" he asks.

The uncomfortable tightness in my chest squeezes a bit tighter.

I manage to swallow. "What is the real reason you sent for me? I'm nothing but a common witch. Not even a highly powerful one, at that."

The king scowls. "You were seen with him yesterday prior to his wedding."

Of course he had Kai followed. I wonder if Captain Mustache was the spy who saw us.

"Because I was with him, you think I turned him into a frog?" I ask flatly.

"Who else do you think would do something like this?"

I keep my voice even. "What would I gain? I already know you don't like me. You've arrested my mother and left me to fend for myself. If you have a spy on Kai, you know I barely see him now. Turning him into a frog would only get me arrested."

The queen reaches out and places her hand over her husband's. She looks older than she should. Her eyes are rimmed red from tears of worry. Did she cry like that when Kai was deployed to war?

"Ask to go to my room," Kai suddenly whispers.

I cough over him, hoping no one else heard his noise. I swallow. "May I see his room? I might be able to find the artifact and use that to find him."

"I don't feel comfortable with her entering *our* room," Princess Genoa says sharply.

There must definitely be something hidden.

King Willard eyes me up and down and then stands. "I will take you myself. Captain Bath, take up the rear."

## Chapter Five

I follow King Willard up another flight of stairs. I slip my hand into my pocket and feel Kai's cold little hand touch mine in what I assume to be a comforting gesture. I feel nauseous and want nothing more than to put my head between my knees and breathe to steady myself as adrenaline bursts through my veins. I'm walking through the castle with the king and his personal guard. I can only hope that he's actually taking me to Kai's room and not somewhere to lock me away forever.

"Tell me what you know of this orb and why it is dangerous." King Willard stops and faces me.

My breath hitches. He's only two steps away, and I can feel the captain behind me. I'm trapped. "What makes you think—"

"I saw your expression change when I said golden orb. What is its significance? Why did you seem surprised?"

I lick my lips and glance back at Captain Bath.

"He won't divulge your secrets. Tell me." The king's voice is commanding.

"I don't have secrets." I face him again. "I have heard of golden orbs. When you said it was enchanted, a golden ball, and that it turned him into a frog . . ." I draw in a shaking breath. "I heard stories when I was a child. There are stories the villagers share as a warning," I start delicately. I know King Willard's disdain for magic in general, so I don't know how well he will take the legend. "What do you know of . . . fairies?"

His eyes darken. "They are dangerous." He knows more. We fought a war against them years ago. But I won't press him.

I rub my arm for comfort. "The villagers who live closest to the woods tell stories to their children to keep them safe. They describe how fairies lure people, especially children, into a ring of toadstools with a golden ball."

He watches me in silent scrutiny.

I continue, "Because fairy rings are portals into the fairy realm. Once you step through, the fairies never let you out. It's possible this orb may be one in the same. Have you seen a fairy recently?" I know it's risky to ask, because it's none of my business if he has, but if he doesn't know Genoa is a fairy, then she's using magic to hide her real identity.

King Willard looks at me with brows knitted. His gaze travels down and back up, searching for the lie he won't see. He finally mutters, "They've been bound away. I haven't seen one since Kaison was born." He reaches out to the door on his right and opens it, then gestures mutely.

I could really use a glass of water. Or an escape plan.

Genoa is definitely a fairy, and no one in the castle

knows.

I enter the bedroom. The walls are painted pale blue, and morning light spills in through sheer white curtains. It's nearly large enough to fit my entire cottage, with a stone fireplace, sitting area with a couch and chair, two wardrobes, and a large bed. I raise my brow at the stack of ten mattresses on top. Didn't Kai say something about fifty mattresses? He must have been exaggerating, but was Princess Genoa insane? I couldn't sleep on a bed that soft—or unsteady, for that matter.

In scanning the room, I notice no golden orb, but crouch beside the bed so I can discreetly reach into my pouch to pull Acorn out to help me search beneath the bed. He eagerly crawls across the rug, pausing a moment because Kai takes the opportunity to leap out of my pocket.

I stifle the urge to yell at him. If he gets us caught, I'm blaming him for everything.

Acorn waits for Kai to hop over. "Let me do the talking, Prince. I only sound like squeaking to the humans. They know they're missing a frog, so we're in trouble if you croak."

They disappear under the bed.

"What more do you know of the golden orb? Or fairies?" King Willard asks.

"Not much, I'm afraid." I look up at the king and shimmy on my knees to look behind the nightstand. "They're incredibly beautiful and have the power to disguise

themselves as human, and one hasn't been seen in decades."
I raise my brows to hint to him that the woman who is now
Kai's wife is the creature I have just described. I don't know
yet if perhaps the king is aware of Genoa being a fairy and is
going along with it.

The king doesn't hint that he's caught on, but it could
all be a guise.

"It's under here!" Acorn says. "And it's definitely
enchanted, because it's glowing."

I walk around to the opposite side of the bed and get on
my hands and knees to bend over. This allows me to talk
without the king seeing me.

Acorn's little eyes briefly reflect the light I discern
coming from the palm-size ball wedged in the corner
against the wall.

"Don't tell them we found it," Kai whispers.

Acorn walks back and forth, sniffing around it. "I'm
already an animal. Maybe I can become human if I touch it.
Be prepared to drag me out from under here!"

"No!" I shout.

He places both tiny hands on the surface of the ball
and . . . nothing happens.

I exhale in relief.

The captain quickly appears from behind the bed. "Is
everything all right?"

"It's my hedgehog," I reply. "He's fine. Just stubborn."

He arches a brow and studies me.

I crouch down again and reach under the bed to grab the ball, but Kai leaps and lands on top of it first. Again, nothing happens. But his weight causes the ball to roll, and just before it makes contact with my hand, I feel a powerful and cold energy radiating from it so intensely I can feel it ache through my hand and into my arm.

I recoil before the gold can make contact with my skin. The orange light coming from it reveals tiny etching that must be in the language of the fairies. They could be fairy runes, as runes are particular to different races and I can't read them.

I quickly reach into my pocket and remove a handkerchief, which is little more than a faded yellow piece of fabric. Luckily, the ball is close enough that I can reach under the bed and grab it with the fabric. I pull it out from beneath the bed just as King Willard steps around the side of the bed.

Holding it in direct sunlight, the markings and glow disappear.

I turn to the king. "I found it. It's more than a gold artifact, though. I can feel its magic."

King Willard raises his eyebrow. "You're good at lying."

My teeth clench. "Tell me again how I could benefit from turning the prince into a frog?"

"Your little rally."

I push off the floor to stand. "First of all, I don't know an enchantment to transform anyone into another living being, because *enchantments* are meant for good. Curses do bad. Second, cursing Prince Kaison would do nothing to help my cause because you would only become more upset with me for turning him. I'm not a fool."

King Willard studies the orb, then me. "You truly believe this to be an artifact of the fairies?"

"There are runes I cannot read. You could have your royal sorcerer examine it. Oh—you don't have one."

"Watch it, little witch."

I bite my lip. It wasn't on purpose. Not entirely. "My apologies. I was being genuine. I forgot he's no longer here. But the university isn't far!"

He looks down his nose at me. "You don't think you're smart enough to figure it out? That is ironic, don't you think? That you might have to visit the very place you despise to help my son?"

"Why do I have to do it?"

He leans closer so I can feel his breath. "You have to fix what you did wrong. Besides, if this is a fairy relic as you claim, you must have the most experience with them."

"How is that?"

"You live near the woods." He nods as if he's decided something. "You must know a lot more about fairies than you are telling me. Either you're on their side, or you cursed him to serve your own purpose. You'll find Kaison, break the spell, and return him to me."

"What?" I cannot help but say in shock. How can he

Amphibian's Kiss

think I'm in cahoots with fairies? And that I would do this to my best friend?

"Do you want your mother out of prison?"

"You'll let her go?" I hesitate to ask.

He shrugs and straightens. "If you bring Kaison back, as a human, yes."

I gnaw on my lip. "If your son was cursed by them, there must be a reason. What if something bad happens?"

"Then all I lose is you." He doesn't hide the curl of his sneer. "You want to prove that you're just as useful as a trained witch, don't you? That magic users don't actually need training and education? Now is your chance. And you're fighting me?"

"It just seems that you're lying to me. This deal feels too good to be true."

"Your feelings are irrelevant." Before I have a chance to respond, he has opened the door to leave.

The captain clears his throat softly and says, "Sir, do you think it's wise to entrust such a big task to . . . *her*?"

"I agree with him." I bend over to grab Acorn and Kai and shove them both in my pouch.

Acorn huffs. "Kai is too soft for my prickles!"

"No," King Willard answers. "Not alone." He looks at the captain before exiting the room.

"You made a mess for yourself," the guard mumbles.

I glare at him. "Clam up." I follow the king.

"This is a bad idea," Acorn says. He's always pessimistic,

but I can't help but agree with him this time. This feels like it was set up for me to fail so the king can arrest me and lock me away too. "You can turn around. Jump out the window. This is ground level. Look! There's an open window right there!"

"Acorn!" I scold. "What good would it do?"

He squeaks back in frustration and nips at my finger before retreating under the flap.

"You really speak with animals?" the whiskered man asks.

I glance over my shoulder at him. "Do you think I'm only speaking to myself?"

He shrugs. "You're a witch."

I roll my eyes.

We enter the throne room with me now awkwardly holding the wrapped golden ball in both hands. The energy it radiates vibrates with a cold tingle. Sort of like when your fingers get too cold from being in the snow and you come inside and they start to wake.

The queen's face finally gains some life when she sees me and what I carry. "You found it?" She actually smiles.

Princess Genoa's eyes snap to me and her pupils dilate. No. She's not looking at me, but at the orb.

If I point out to the king that she's a fairy and this is hers, what will happen? He hated fairies long ago. I cannot believe he is willingly on her side. So what would the fairy want with Kai being a frog? An overwhelming rush tingles through my joints and I hear something warn that there is no one else Kai can trust but me. If I give this ball to the fairy, she can accomplish her task. If I take it to the university and ask someone else to figure this out, chances are they would see my inadequacies, take him, and ask me to go home. I will have to pretend I don't care what happens to him.

I hold the ball a little closer and then silently slip it into my pouch.

King Willard takes the hands of his wife. "Elowyn will find Kaison and return him to us."

"Oh?" She blinks and looks over at me.

"Yes, in exchange for her mother's freedom."

I grip the strap of my bag. "And he will grant us immunity against the law requiring testing and allow us to live our lives without fines or punishment."

The king slowly raises an eyebrow but doesn't say anything to counter.

Genoa's lips tighten.

"And one more thing," I add.

"More?" King Willard's voice grits.

"I refuse to be the only one looking for Kai. You must also send out your soldiers because I will not accept any guilt if we cannot find him. I am only one person and cannot cover the entire kingdom."

King Willard snorts a laugh. "Why would you search for him at all with an arrangement like that? Where is the guarantee you will find him and not just find somewhere in the woods to hide for a month?"

"I told you that you should have run when you had the chance," Acorn grumbles.

I pat my pocket, essentially bopping him on the rear end, silencing him.

He grunts before burrowing deep—and I assume facing his prickles out toward me for good measure. "He has a point."

I shake my head. "I have *everything* to lose if I can't help Kai."

The king slides his arm around his wife, lips tight. "Then you have until the autumn comes."

I nod. My stomach churns.

"And Captain Bath will accompany you." King Willard sits.

I glance at the fool with the mustache.

He bows to our king. "If that is what you wish, sire. I will need to gather my supplies before we leave."

I raise my hands. "I do not need a royal escort."

"Think of it as my own assurance you'll fulfil your end of the deal," King Willard says.

I flash him a respectful smile, curtsey stiffly, and turn to face the soldier. "Then I shall see you in a couple of hours," I say through gritted teeth.

"Can't wait." He meets me with just as much enthusiasm.

I drop my smile, turn, and exit the throne room, then the castle, and storm down the road.

With no one around, Kai finally speaks. "This is going to be more difficult than I thought. Did you feel that Genoa is up to something?"

"Yes," I say a bit more firmly than intended. "She wouldn't stop staring at the orb when I came in with it, and she is definitely a fairy." I look down at him to see he is poking his head out of the pouch. "You didn't notice anything when you married her?"

He sighs. "I don't . . . I don't know. I saw a glow, but I thought it was just because she's beautiful."

"She's got a glamour." I run my hand over my face. "I still don't understand why I couldn't just hand you over to them right there."

"Is that what you really want? You can give me to Garrett when he arrives. I trust him."

"No. I need to help you." I sigh and slowly let out a growl to release my frustration until the tightness in my chest loosens. "Wait, the mustache man's first name is Garrett?"

Kai nods.

I lick my lips. "We won't go to the university. We need to find the fairies. One of them is bound to know how to help."

"Feel better?" Acorn asks.

"A little."

Kai clears his throat. "Then I guess we just find a fairy

ring?"

I kick a rock. "Easy for you to say. And now we have a stupid guard to take with us. Did you see the mustache? It looks like he has a caterpillar stuck under his nose!"

Kaison laughs.

I even get a little squeak from Acorn.

## Chapter Six

"I can't believe we are going to go looking for fairies. Do you have a death wish?" Acorn sits on his counter cushion, half-rolled up, arms resting on his pudgy belly. He tracks my movements with his eyes.

"You don't have to come," I reply and crouch to get whatever food is stored in the lower cupboards. "You can keep an eye on the place."

He licks his lips and wipes his eyes. "And who will keep you safe? The frog?"

I laugh and set the preserved fruit and jam on the counter with everything else. "Acorn, darling, you've never had to protect me from anything."

"I might now that two strange men are joining us!"

"Technically only one is actually a man." I glance at Kai.

He sits on the window ledge, just . . . staring at me.

I clear my throat. "Because the other is a frog."

He must be lost in thought because he still doesn't respond.

I shake my head and grab my storage of nuts I collected last fall and the dried meat I keep as backup for Acorn in emergencies. It's not the season yet for any tree nuts, so I only have what is left from my winter storage. I also only have half a loaf of sourdough. That's enough for me for a couple of days, but now that I have to feed Captain Bath. I am not about to call him by his title for the length of our journey. But what is his real name? Something with a G? I'll just call him Whiskers. Now that he's tagging along, I have to double the amount of food to take, unless he has packed his own. And in all honesty, I have no idea how long it might actually take us to find a fairy ring in the first place. If luck finally decides to join me, perhaps we can find one tomorrow.

I've never traveled beyond the city. My heart is racing, unsure if what I'm planning on packing is too little or too much of what we need. What if there is rain or snow? Of course, it *is* the beginning of summer, not quite the solstice, so the only way I would encounter a snowstorm is if we somehow end up in the mountains, and I have *no* desire to visit with giants or trolls.

I stop with a bundle of dried apples in one hand, a jar of peaches under my arm, and the half loaf of bread in my hand. "Kai? How much food does a man even eat?"

At me saying his name, he turns his head, finally acknowledging my presence.

"How much food do I need to bring for the captain?" I restate.

Kai makes a movement I could almost consider a shrug. "Soldiers eat a lot of things like meat and cheese when we're traveling and fighting. We need a lot of energy. I don't know. Healthy portion sizes?"

I don't understand what that means, but at least he's talking now. "I'll get Pancho and the wagon so we can unpack the things to sell and replace them with what we'll need." I place everything back down into the growing mess. "I don't know if the canopy is designed for travel. I wish you had hands to help."

"If I did have hands, you wouldn't be in this mess to begin with," Kai grumbles.

Acorn gasps and unrolls. "You feel bad?"

"Of course I do. I've been thinking, Elowyn, that you should just take me and the ball to the university and let them deal with it."

I smile at him. "It's a bit too late for that now. I made a promise that I would help you, so you're stuck with me. Why don't you tell me what you know of that soldier who reluctantly volunteered to join us?" I cross the room and get on my knees to look under my mother's bed for any bags.

"He's one of my father's most trusted men. He was stationed with me last month at the battle of The Wall. He's a skilled swordsman and horseback rider."

None of that is actually helpful information.

"You said you trust him?" I specify.

"As a soldier, absolutely."

I wrap my fingers around something and drag it out from under the bed. It's a bundled-up bag, which will be perfect for my clothes.

Kai's words dawn on me and I turn to him. "As a soldier? But not as a man?"

He sighs. "I don't know anything about him as a man. We have different social circles."

A loud knock on my door jars me from my thoughts and I realize I've successfully pulled almost everything out and set them on the counter, but not actually packed a single thing.

"It's the knight," Acorn announces. He's leaning his tiny hands against a window pane.

I survey my home in its state of organized chaos and have half a mind to pretend I'm not home. However, ignoring the man won't help, so I reluctantly open the door. "You've arrived just in time to help."

I watch Whiskers as his gaze drifts past my face and one of his eyebrows rises slowly. Judgement oozes off of him. "I see that."

"Ha ha," I answer sarcastically. I cross the room to my wardrobe and remove the only clothing I have—two shirts, one skirt as I'm wearing the other, and a single pair of boots. Everything else is Mother's.

Whiskers steps inside. "I always wondered what it would look like in here."

I glance over my shoulder to find him studying my wall of ingredients. "Is it as evil as you imagined?" I shove everything in the pack I dragged out from under the bed.

I'm pretty sure it used to be my father's.

Whiskers taps a jar of squirrel bones. "I expected more bones, to be honest."

I roll my eyes and drop the bag beside the door. "I don't have enough food to last more than a couple of days. If we leave tomorrow, that will give me time to bake some more bread and trade for cheese with the neighbors."

He leans his backside against the workbench, crosses his ankles and his arms. "We can just purchase our meals or supplies along the way."

I look him up and down. "Do you see how I live? I don't have any way to afford that and will not be able to earn money while we travel."

His expression remains perfectly stoic. "I think you are overestimating how much time this will take. I do not plan on being gone with you for three months, so you need to admit to what you've done with him and resolve the problem."

My chest tightens and I quickly scan the countertop for Kai, but he is nowhere to be seen. I'm still conflicted about whether or not to tell Whiskers that I actually found Kai last night, and if Kai wanted to be seen, he wouldn't have hidden.

I suck in a deep breath and face the king's guard. "I had nothing to do with Kai's curse. I don't have to prove anything to you."

"It's *Prince Kaison* to you." His mustache twitches as

his lips pull into a sneer. "But if it makes you feel better, King Willard gave me some money." He pats a pouch tied to his belt, which jingles with the sound of coins clashing together.

As much as I hate to admit that I'm relieved, I am. Who knows how long we'll be gone?

"Good." I gesture both hands toward the door. "Make yourself useful. I have a donkey we can take with us, and a wagon. Why don't you go hook him up? That is, if you know how." I intend every ounce of dripping attitude I throw at him. And it gives me a way to kick him out of my home for a little while.

Whiskers' eyes narrow. "I brought my horse. We can take him."

I raise my brow. "I need more supplies than what a horse can carry."

"He has saddlebags." As if that's supposed to explain how it can carry pots, dishes, poultices and potions, and everything else I'm going to take. Not to mention, the idea of sharing a saddle with a complete stranger sounds like absolute torture. Whiskers sighs. "You really want to take the wagon, don't you?"

"Yes."

He shakes his head before stalking from the kitchen and outside.

I rest both hands on the counter as I lean to peer through the window overlooking the small donkey pen.

"These are going to be the longest days of my life." I put one hand on my hip. "You know, at some point he's going to figure out you're here." I look down at where Kai is hiding, behind my pot of dill weed.

He croaks. "I'm not ready for that yet."

"Don't you think it will be better for us both if you tell him now than if we wait? Won't he be more convinced I did this to you?"

"I don't care." Kai hops out from where he had hidden himself.

I shake my head. "I find him terribly annoying."

I turn and collect my smaller pot. It should hold enough food for two people and will take up less space in the wagon. I add the lone sweet potato I have inside of the pot and set it on the edge of the counter.

"Do you think he'll hurt us?" Acorn asks timidly.

I shake my head. "I don't think he's going to cause any harm. He can't, based on our deal with the king. He's just . . . serious."

"Seriously annoying," Acorn chimes in.

That makes me laugh.

Acorn folds his hands. "I don't trust him."

"Is it the mustache?" I grin.

Acorn tilts his head. "Likely," he concludes. "Very caterpillar."

I see Whiskers through the window approaching the front door. "You know, I can't remember his first name, so

I've just nicknamed him Whiskers." I have deliberately waited until he has pushed door open, allowing him to hear.

He frowns and points to his chest. "Who is Whiskers? Me?"

I barely try to hide my smile. "I couldn't remember your name."

His blue eyes darken. "Whiskers is a name you give a cat. I'm not a cat." His frown deepens—which looks anything but intimidating.

"It's the mustache." I stick my finger under my nose.

He heaves a sigh and shakes his head. "My name is Garrett."

"That's . . . a name." Resisting the urge to smile, as he is clearly already perturbed, I cross to the sink and fill a cup with water, then take a big drink and wipe the back of my hand across my mouth. "We can start loading the wagon. I need to pack some blankets and the food." I set my cup on the table, then turn and find a long container with a wooden lid. "In the meantime, I need you to go to the apple tree and get as many caterpillars as possible. Get some leaves too. Please? Whiskers?" I show every tooth I can in my biggest smile.

He doesn't immediately move to take the container.

"The caterpillars are for Acorn. My hedgehog." I gesture to where he is watching from the counter. "He'll need to eat as we travel and he loves caterpillars."

Whiskers snatches the container from me and I turn my

back to organize what is coming and what can stay behind.

I hear a crash and whip around to see Garrett still standing in place, but my glass—and water—are now on the floor.

"Meow," he says, then turns and leaves the house.

I blink after him. "Did he just knock my cup off of the counter?"

"You *did* call him a cat," Kai states.

I roll my eyes and crouch to pick up and examine the glass to ensure it didn't break.

Acorn is in a fit of giggles. "I think I might like him after all!"

Chapter Seven

Once the wagon is cleared of my wares, we repack it with what we are going to need while traveling: the pot, my bag of clothes, and spare blankets, along with Garrett's large pack. I've also buffered the jars of fruit preserves and canned vegetables with packages of dry ingredients. I'm a witch, after all, and who knows what we might encounter where potions, salves, or poultices can assist?

Garrett drops the last of my firewood behind the bench of the wagon. I'll need to start chopping more to get stored for the coming winter.

The sun beats down on my black hair, which I lift up off my neck in an attempt to cool down and fan my face with my hand.

Whiskers removes the container of caterpillars from his pocket and holds it inches from my face. "Is this enough?"

I lean back to accept it and get a better look. "Perfect! Thank you." I offer him a genuine smile this time. I choose two of them and set the container in the last basket on the shelf. "Come in for some lunch." I nudge my head toward the house.

His gaze drifts to the caterpillars in my hand. "Do I have

to?"

"What, you aren't a fan of garlic caterpillar orzo?" I sniff the caterpillars as if I'm choosing a rot-free vegetable.

Whiskers tilts his head. "I can never tell when you're serious."

Blinking in disbelief, I try leaning my head forward. "Do you honestly believe I eat caterpillars?"

"You *are* a witch."

"Not a bog witch!" I roll my eyes and throw my hands up in the air. "Four winds. He believes I eat bugs!"

Behind me, I swear I hear him chuckle, but when I look back, his expression hasn't changed.

Acorn chitters and squeaks with excitement when he notices the caterpillars I bring in. I set one of them in front of him and the other behind the pot of dill for Kai. Acorn scurries over, snatches the pudgy creature with his little claws, and bites in immediately.

"You're going to let it sit right there on the counter and eat?" Whiskers asks as he walks in.

I raise my brow. "You don't have to watch him. Besides, he was here first."

"I can't believe I'm arguing about a rodent," he mutters.

Acorn squeaks. "Who is he calling a rodent?"

"You," I reply.

"I what?" Whiskers asks.

I grin. "You called him a rodent. Now he's going to hate you. We should eat lunch before we leave."

"We can eat while we travel. We should get moving and cover some ground before night falls. And you should probably let me in on your plan on how we're moving forward."

I tap my chin. "We're going to find a fairy ring. I would like to stop by Samuel's house to ask him where to find one. They aren't just anywhere, and nowhere near here. He used to tell me stories all the time about how he had discovered some."

Whiskers lets out a breath that causes his cheeks to puff up with air. "And you don't know how to find one? I thought there was a way to lure fairies."

I shrug. "I've heard you can use enchanted milk or something, but why not go to someone who has actually seen one? That's got to be quicker than wandering the woods. Don't you think?"

He leans his arm on the counter, leaning toward me. "Look, I don't want to be here either. I just want to find the prince and get back to doing what I should be."

"Watching the king sleep?" I ask.

The soldier smirks and his mustache moves. "My job is more important than keeping the royal family safe while they're sleeping."

"Yes. So important they sent you to babysit me."

"At least I will get to help save the prince." He moves around my kitchen, swiping the last of my bread and a jar of marmalade. "Let's go."

Licking my lips, I carefully collect Acorn, deposit him in his typical spot in my pouch, and collect Kai with my free hand. He goes in my skirt pocket, which is a safer place for him.

Acorn pokes his head out. "Think we'll be back fast?"

"You can still stay," I reply.

"No! You two are the most entertaining people I've ever met! I want to see how this plays out!" His nose twitches in familiar excitement.

"I can't believe you find this entertaining," Kai says.

"Did you hear someone?" Whiskers asks, glancing around.

My brows furrow. "Hear what?"

"Hm. Nothing. Are you ready?"

Had he understood Kai? No. He must have heard him croak.

I turn, bite my bottom lip, and scan the room one more time. I feel like there are so many more things I should grab. Do I actually need more ingredients? Perhaps I should take the crystals? Who knows when I might need more plants?

He clears his throat.

"I'm ready. Sorry." I walk out the door, closing it behind me.

Something about that sound feels more hollow than usual. Like I might not be coming back, or if I do, everything will be different. I was comfortable in my life with my mother. Losing her forced me to step out and fend for myself, but I have also pushed everyone else away so I don't have to feel that pain ever again. I don't know what to expect from here, where to go, or how to help Kai. All I know is if I don't, both of us are going to end up miserable for the rest of our lives.

I won't let that happen to him.

Garrett sits by my side as I unnecessarily hold the reins of Pancho's bridle and giving him a little snap to go. "Go ahead," I command.

The wagon lurches forward.

I have never noticed how small the bench of the wagon is until I had to wedge myself next to the massive soldier. Sitting down, my shoulders don't even reach his, and when I look down at our legs, his thigh is nearly one and a half of mine. Okay, that's pure speculation, but they're enormous. His forearms are even muscled, and I find myself wondering what they look like when he grips a sword.

"What do you do all day?" I thought I said it in my mind, but Garrett looks down at me and I realize I've accidentally said it out loud.

"I have a strict schedule. Wake up before dawn, bathe, stretch . . ."

I regret having asked him.

". . . walk the grounds for potential breaches, check in with the night guards and captains, plan rotations with the day captains, and check in with the king's schedule. If there isn't anything that requires me to be in the castle at the king's side, I switch off with the other king's guards so I can train new soldiers."

I look across him to the sword dangling off the side of the wagon. "You train them in sword fighting?"

Whiskers nods. "And hand-to-hand combat."

"Braggart," Kai mutters.

"Hm?" Whiskers asks.

Luckily, the word sounds close to *Ribbit*, but I feel obligated to speak before Kai can add any other snide remarks. "Are you any good?" I say, raising an eyebrow, knowing that to be alongside the king he must be.

He smirks. "The best. Why do you think he sent me with you?"

"As punishment?"

Garrett's lips actually pull into a smile and he snorts a laugh, then shakes his head. "It feels like that."

"At least we're on the same page. I feel the same way about you." I straighten my spine and refocus my attention forward. "Why would the king send you and not one of Kai's bodyguards?"

Garrett chuckles. "Prince Kaison doesn't have one. One of us keeps an eye on him at all times, but he can hold his own. What about you? What do you do?"

I didn't expect him to reciprocate the interaction and can't help but look at him from the corner of my eye. "Do you actually want to know? Or are you just making small talk to feel better about yourself?"

He shrugs. "If we're going to be together for at least a week, by the looks of things, I should probably know something about you. Shouldn't I? I shared my daily life with you."

"Your schedule," I correct. "I still only know you're a guard."

Whiskers tilts his head and shifts on the seat so he's facing me the best he can. It only makes his knee lean into mine. "My name is Garrett Bath. Yes, like water and soap. I am twenty-five years of age and I'm excellent in long and short sword combat. I grew up in the streets, boxing to make money and earn a reputation so I could apply to be a soldier of the king. I found a captain and basically followed him for a month until he finally admitted my worth and took me on as a squire. When I saved his life during an assassination attempt on the king, he started training me."

I force myself into the most unamused expression I can muster. "That is the quickest summary of someone's life I've ever heard." He grew up in the streets? "So you don't have a family?" Ugh, why am I asking for more information about him?

Because what else are we going to do on this long ride?

Garrett runs his fingers through his brown hair and the waves spring back into place. I silently wonder if he puts in fancy product. I sometimes make beauty products to help with hair care, lotion, paste to clean teeth, and so forth, but it's not a passion of mine. I wonder if there's a market for soldiers.

"I, uh, don't know," Garrett admits. "I have vague memories of them, but I don't know what happened." He shrugs. "You have a mother. What about your father?"

My teeth clench as anger burns through me. It's instantaneous and bitter. It's not the same anger I feel toward Kai. Kai's feeling is betrayal while the anger toward my father is seething. "He walked out when I was young. I think five or six? He said he could make a better life without the burden of a peculiar child like me."

"I don't get that."

I look at Garrett, but his gaze is on the road. "What do you mean?"

"Well, your mother is a magic user. He clearly chose to marry her, or at least have a child with her. Why choose a magical person and get upset about having a magical child? Seems like he was blaming you for choices he made. A child is an easy thing to blame."

I'd never looked back on the incident through the eyes of an adult. If my father was doing something wrong, of course his narcissistic self would blame a child. Children can't fight. That thought made my chest ache.

Maybe it really wasn't my fault my father left.

He must have made poor choices and turned on me because it was easier to do than admit his own faults.

I reach my hand up and rub my chest. "It's interesting how we're actually pretty similar," I say.

"Oh? Because we had rough childhoods?"

I rub my arm. "That and we've fought for everything we have learned. We want better lives and we're willing to do what we need in order to do so."

He snorts and leans back, spreading his legs a bit to intentionally push my knees to the side. "You're fighting against the throne. I want to help it. We are not similar."

"I'm fighting to practice magic without the control of a law." It's my turn to face him, and I have no issues pushing against his thigh with my knees. "Not even that. I don't even mind having to get a license, but to be required to attend a university and then take an expensive exam on top of that seems preposterous when every other job doesn't require a piece of paper validating their experience. What harm has my magic ever caused? I help farmers kill pests to preserve their crops. I make medicines."

Whiskers' eyebrow lifts. "Your enchantment turned the prince into a frog," he counters.

"Four winds! The orb is a fairy relic!" I nearly shout.

"So you claim."

The prickle of anger flares up the back of my neck and I ball my hands into fists. "You can walk the entire way if you wish."

Garrett straightens and slowly lets a breath out through his nose. "I have seen what sorcerers and witches can do during war. I have seen what battle magic can do."

"There is good in magic too," I insist. "I can show you

while you're with me and you can take whatever information you want to the king. You'll see."

"I doubt it," he mutters.

"You're more of a pessimist than Acorn." I roll my eyes. "Pancho, stop. We're here."

# Chapter Eight

The farm we have arrived at is a familiar sight. Though I haven't been here in a year, it's just as green and rich as ever. A man working in the field between us and the small farmhouse straightens. He removes his hat to wipe his forehead and spots me.

My heart pangs and I offer a weak wave before I hop down from the wagon.

Samuel's wrinkled face breaks into a grin and he waves his hat. "Elowyn!" he shouts.

Relief floods through me. I feel guilty for keeping my distance from him as he attempts to run to me through the rows of straw, leaning heavily on his cane as he does so. His leg must be getting worse. I should have been helping him.

I gather up my skirts and hurry to meet him. "Samuel, you don't need to rush."

"Did you get the squash I dropped off for you in the fall?" he calls.

"Yes. They were delicious." I catch up to him and grasp one wrinkled hand as his other holds his cane. "It was very kind of you to bring those out to me. I . . . I'm sorry I didn't reciprocate."

He waves his cane, shaking his head dismissively. "Stop. You have been fending on your own. Giving you some food is the least I can do. I wish I had done more."

I smile softly.

His sun-worn skin is speckled with dark spots, but his blue eyes still sparkle, though they're more gray now. "Who is your friend?" He nudges his chin toward the wagon and lifts his brows in a teasing manner.

I don't need to look and instead heave a sigh. "That would be Captain Bath. He's one of the king's guard."

"Ah?" He grins. "You are courting?"

"Court . . . no!" I clear my throat. "No. He's . . . helping me." I slip my arm into his and turn him around to walk toward his home. I lower my voice. "We need to talk about the fairies."

"Cherries?"

"Fairies," I say a bit louder.

He stops dead in his tracks, his brightness dropping, and gives me a serious look. "Why would you ask about fairies?"

"It's a long story. But I have to find one. I need a fairy ring."

He shakes his head and pulls his arm away. "No. No. I will not help you find one."

"Samuel, please. It's urgent. It's a task for the king."

"To find fairies?" He nearly throws his hat as he energetically exclaims, "Why in the four winds could you possibly need a fairy?"

"Is everything all right, Father?" someone calls from the farmhouse.

I glance and see one of his sons now heading toward us. I had hoped this would be a quick discussion, but it's clearly going to take a bit of time.

I feel Garrett's presence before I hear his deep voice.

"Good day. I am Captain Bath. You may call me Garrett, if you wish." He holds his large hand out toward the old man.

Samuel accepts it with little hesitation. "I am Samuel."

"You know Elowyn?" Garrett places both hands behind his back, looking very much like a soldier.

"Yes. Since she was a tiny troll."

I cannot resist a smile, knowing Samuel uses the term as one of endearment. He used to call me his "little troll" because Kai and I would stick weeds and twigs in our hair and clothes to make us look like trolls when we played in his canal.

Garrett offers Samuel a polite smile. "She's told me good things about you and said you might be able to help us." I'm not surprised he can lie so easily.

By now, Samuel's youngest son, Hayden, has arrived. He's about five years older than me and was a surprise after their other children had grown—he's the same age as his oldest sister's son. He's a farmer's son, so he's muscled as one but is still smaller than Garrett.

He looks the soldier up and down and steps up behind his father. "Is everything all right?"

"Long story short," I begin and all of the men look at me, "the king has asked Garrett and me to find a fairy ring. We need to find and speak with a fairy."

"You know that's dangerous," Hayden mutters.

"Of course I do."

"If you step into a fairy ring, you can't come back," Samuel says forcefully. "I can tolerate your grieving and stubbornness. You get that from your mother. But you are needed here."

"I'm not stepping into one. I just need to send them a message and request a discussion." I resist the urge to reply that his family has survived just fine without me.

"The fairies can't cross over," Samuel adds.

That's not entirely true. I know that Princess Genoa is a fairy, even if her glamor prevents anyone non-magical from seeing her true identity.

"I know very little of fairy rings," Garrett says. "Have you ever seen one?"

I've already told him and nearly interrupt with annoyance to re-explain it, but he clears his throat. He's using this opportunity to gain whatever information we can. Maybe he's not so annoying.

Samuel begins, "They are rings of mushrooms found in meadows in the woods. They don't look like much at first, which is why people disappear in the woods. It is easy to step in one without realizing it. I have seen five in my lifetime."

"These only grow in the woods?"

He bobs his head up and down. "Fairies keep to themselves."

Garrett rubs his chin. "And yet you say you've seen five?" He turns and looks around at the farm. "That's hard to believe, seeing as they're so rare."

"Are you calling me a liar?" Samuel huffs.

"I'm only saying, as one soldier to another, we like to stretch stories, don't we?" Garrett offers a small smile.

Samuel's eyes scrunch. "How'd you know I was a soldier?"

Garrett gestures to Samuel's leg. "War wound? You stand like a soldier, in spite of your age. And your tattoo." His smile broadens. "Blue Wing?"

Samuel's frown slowly spreads into a big grin and he claps Garrett on the shoulder. "You are observant." He taps his nose with his finger. "Come in for some coffee." He turns and leans on Hayden.

I glance at Garrett. "We don't really have the time—"

"Nonsense. Lynette will be furious if she doesn't get to see you," he insists.

I let them get ahead before I place my fists on my hips and face Garrett. "Tattoo?"

He holds up his left wrist, revealing a tattoo on it. It's a black horizontal line with a raven silhouette in the middle and fine line swirls above and below. "I was in the Raven branch. The solid line and swirls with that tiny symbol in the middle"—he points—"indicate my ranking."

"Every soldier has a tattoo?" I don't know why it's only just dawned on me that Kai's tattoo on his wrist is because he's a soldier. I've seen the wolf symbol and the curved line above it. I recall asking him years ago why he got it, but he was so dismissive about it I never asked again.

Garrett nods. "There is an entire ceremony. You get your branch tattooed first, then whatever ranking you accomplish is added as you go."

"What does the raven represent, then?"

"Ah. I'm..." He tilts his head, eyes darting to me as if he is debating being honest. He finally shrugs. "I am a spy."

I look him up and down. "That makes sense for why the king wanted you to babysit me."

"I suppose." He turns his attention forward.

"What is the wolf branch?"

Garrett's lip tugs and he looks at me from the corner of his eyes. "Kai's? He never told you?"

I frown and look away, pretending not to be interested in the answer. The tattoo makes me wonder if he has more hidden beneath his uniform. "We should follow Samuel."

He smirks. "If I didn't know any better, I would say you were proud of me for how I handled that."

I begin walking. "I would have gotten him to talk."

"Eventually." He follows. "The wolves are usually the

front line. They're the most fiercely trained."

I want to ask more about this and wonder why Kai wouldn't tell me such things. Of course, it may be because he didn't want me to worry. He had to fight on the front line in every battle?

A pang grips my chest when I enter the familiar, rundown home. Although Samuel's children are all grown now and the space isn't cluttered with sleeping rolls and toys, there is an area of the home for broken furniture I'm certain Samuel has promised he will repair. I nervously remove my hat and hang it on a hook inside of the door.

His wife, Lynette, beams at me through almond eyes as she pushes the wrapping on her head back off her eyebrows. "Elowyn, is that you? Oh goodness, dear! It's been ages!" She shuffles away from the counter where she has been preparing some sort of food.

I don't hesitate to step forward and wrap her in my arms. "Lynette. I'm so sorry I haven't visited." I don't want to admit it's because of my own selfish loneliness.

"Oh hush. It's good to see you now." She steps back and places a hand gnarled with arthritis on my cheek. "You are beautiful as always."

I laugh tightly. "Let me help you get some coffee going." I don't hesitate to leave her behind, because I want to help and give her a break. I get the pot from where it sits on the corner of the counter. "How are your kids?"

"Lynette, dear, sit down and let Elowyn take care of it."

"She is a guest in our house. I'll do no such thing." She swats playfully at Samuel's outstretched hand.

"I can help. You both sit." Hayden guides his mother to her chair and turns to me with a smile and shake of his head. "I'm glad you came to visit. It's been a while since I've seen Mother smile so big."

I set the pot on the stove and the corner of my lip tugs. "I wish I had visited before now. It's just been difficult, you know?"

"No, I don't. I can't imagine what it would be like to be alone." He chuckles.

"I can't imagine living in a house of eight kids," I counter.

We both laugh and my heart swells with the old, familiar feeling I've missed.

Hayden organizes biscuits and cookies on a tray. "We would have helped, you know."

"I know you tried," I confess. "I just felt so betrayed I didn't want to trust anyone ever again." I flinch, remembering that Kai is currently resting in my pocket and can hear everything I say. It's not new information, but I feel bad letting him overhear just how alone I truly was.

"I'm sure Kai had a reason," Hayden says in a gentle tone. "He had to have. He loved you and your mother so much, there's no way he acted without cause. Did you ever ask him?"

I shake my head and pull my black braid over my

shoulder. "I never did. I was hurt."

"And it was easier pushing everyone away?"

I exhale heavily through my nose and glance back at Garrett, who is now seated and chatting with the elderly couple. "I thought it was at the time. I'm already such an outcast, I didn't care if anyone never saw me. I poured my time into trying to get my mother released and when that didn't work, I had to refocus on getting enough money and supplies to last the winter. It sounds pathetic talking about it now."

"Nah, it's not pathetic." Hayden picks up the plate of snacks. "I'm sorry you felt like you had to be alone." He offers me a gentle smile, which I return.

"When I get back from this assignment, I'll make sure not to stay away like before."

"Good." He nods and carries the tray to the small table between his parents.

I finish with the coffee and pour it into five mismatched mugs. I doubt they've ever had anything that matched. I carry two at a time over and set them beside the couple, and Garrett stands to fetch the other three before I can.

As he passes me, he says, "Sit."

I sit on a cushion on the floor with my back to the glowing fireplace.

"Do you still have that little creature?" Lynette asks.

"Acorn?" I grin and carefully pull the sleeping ball of prickles from his pouch. "He's as healthy as ever."

His little body tightens in silent protest, so I put him back where he belongs.

"Elowyn, why are you on the floor?" Whiskers asks when he comes back and stops at my side.

As if I didn't have to look up at him when I'm standing, now I have to look even higher. "I like the floor?"

"Ladies sit in chairs," he insists. He hands Samuel one of the mugs, then holds his free hand out to me.

"I don't mind," I insist, but I feel heat on my cheeks when he doesn't move. I clear my throat, accept his hand, and am mildly surprised how easily he lifts me to my feet. "Thank you." I swallow.

He gives me a mug of coffee and takes my previous spot, leaving his chair open for me.

I glance at the others and don't miss all of their big smiles as I sit. "Samuel, you were telling Garrett about the mushroom rings."

He frowns, lowering the coffee from his lips. "Fairies are evil things."

"You were telling me where you saw one so we could avoid it," Garrett adds. He sips his coffee, and I wonder if I'm going to see it dripping from his mustache when he lowers the cup. Somehow, there isn't a drop on it. Now I can't tease him.

"In my youth, we used to jump from the cliffs of Mirror Falls." Samuel leans back in his chair as he's caught up in the memory.

I've heard of that place. There are tales that the water has healing properties. Mother and I were planning on collecting some for various tonics. People used to visit it to bathe or drink the water to heal their ailments. I don't know if they still do.

"We would race to see who could make it up and down the fastest," Samuel continues. "I would always cut up the northwest edge. Everyone thought it was more dangerous because the trees hug that side, but I found that if I ran around from the west, there was an enormous meadow and no trees until I reached those by the waterfall. That's where I found the fairy ring." He frowns and leans forward. "You stay away from that, Elowyn."

"I only want to visit the falls," I lie. "I need some of the water for new healing potions I want to try."

"Good." He nods and drinks his coffee.

Garrett shifts the conversation to Samuel's battle memories. I would love to sit all day, but after a bathroom break, Garrett is ready to go.

As we head for the wagon, Samuel calls after us, "Oh, and watch out for the toll bridge!"

"Thank you!" I wave back.

"So we head to the falls." Garrett unnecessarily smooths his mustache.

"Yes, sir." I give him a salute with my right hand, which makes him roll his eyes. He's back to the Garrett I met this morning.

"If you're going to salute, at least do it correctly." He stands at attention, spine straight. His left arm goes up with his palm facing outward and fingertips touching his forehead. This shows off the tattoo.

I clap slowly. "Impressive. Can we go now?"

He relaxes his stance, cheeks flushing a light pink, and quietly walks to the wagon. I've made him blush!

I climb up, and only after I'm seated does Garrett climb in beside me. "Go ahead, Pancho." I turn to Garrett. "Aren't you nervous about being seen with me? It's easy for everyone to recognize who I am." I point to my eye.

"Hadn't noticed," he lies. "And no. That's why I'm still in my soldier's uniform."

"Ah. It looks like you're arresting me." I nod.

"What? No." He actually looks offended.

The light gray clouds above open and release a sprinkle of water. I pull my hat on and tilt it forward to shield my face from the rain. I glance at Whiskers. "You should have brought a hat to protect your perfect chestnut hair."

He glances up, as if he could see his own hair, and then smiles. "I suppose that's true. I would never wear one though. Soldiers wear helmets. Where did you get that thing anyway?"

"Thing? I'll have you know this is my favorite piece of clothing." I stroke the brim of my hat. "My mother got it for me some years ago. I pin plants to it while I'm out in the woods."

"And you never poke your own head?" Raindrops gather on his mustache and dislodge as he speaks. He reaches up and dries it with his hand.

I laugh. "I don't pin them while it's on my head."

"I meant if they come loose," he replies, flustered and rolling his eyes.

"Do you ever poke yourself with *that* thing?" I jab my finger against the pin holding his cloak.

He raises a brow. "Yes."

I sigh. "You're far too serious."

"Okay, okay." He holds up both hands in surrender. "I apologize."

"You should be saying something funny! Like '*Well, you're too silly.*'" I realize as I'm coaching him that Kai would have bantered back. I'm trying to get him to respond the way Kai would, and my heart pangs.

Garrett pushes his lips to one side, making his mustache shift too. "Let's just . . . focus on the task at hand, yes?"

Yes. I should be more focused on getting Kai back to himself than flirting with a knight who will never want to see me after this. "We should get there tomorrow," I reply, turning my attention forward.

We will find the fairies, break Kai's spell, and . . . I will go back to being alone.

## Chapter Nine

The sun has settled in the blanket of trees, and the warm glow of the sun lingers. I am grateful the sun's light has lengthened. Winter is so depressing. In just a couple of weeks will be the summer solstice and then the sun will be bright even longer and I won't have to hide in my cottage as long.

"We will set up a fire here." He's crouched and dragging foliage away from a rocky area with his fingers. As much as I hate it, I have to rely on Garrett's knowledge to set up our camp.

Feeling awkward standing and watching him, I open the back door of the wagon. "I'll get things for dinner."

As I go to climb in, I notice Garrett reach out like he's going to help me in, but I don't need his assistance doing something I do every day. He catches himself when I look him up and down and clears his throat. "I'll take the logs and get the fire going, then. Unless you wish to start it with some magic?" His whiskers tug in a playful smirk.

"Don't you have a striking stone or something useful?" I counter.

He chuckles and climbs into the wagon behind me. The

space was always tight with me alone. It's not a large wagon for hauling hay or families. It's a simple wagon, just for me. And with Garrett in my space I realize just how small it really is. His presence swallows the little space I have to move. When he reaches to get the wood, his body presses against my back.

My throat feels tight. "Maybe I should get out so you can get the wood easier," I offer.

He straightens, holding three logs. "There's no need. I've got it." He backs up out of the wagon. "Oh, what meat did you pack?"

"None."

He raises both brows. "What? At all?"

"I don't eat meat." When he continues to stare at me, I add, "With my ability to talk to animals, I can't kill them to eat them. Can you imagine trying to explain to one why I have to kill it? *I'm sorry, beautiful little bunny, but I have to end your life so I can eat your flesh.*" I shudder and gag.

"Point taken." He nudges the door shut.

I feel like I can finally breathe.

"Finally. I thought he would never leave you alone!" I feel Kai wriggle before he pops his head out. "I'm dying in here! It's hot and uncomfortable and dry. Why do I feel so dry?"

"You're a frog," I whisper. "Frogs spend time in water. I did get a water pouch. Let me get you a bowl set up. Acorn should be waking soon too, so you and he can go get some dinner together if you want. I do have a few caterpillars, but I don't know if we should save them." I set what I have back down and take a small bowl out.

"Do you like him?"

I blanch and face him. "Excuse me?"

"Garrett," he clarifies. His eyes seem lower in his head, like he's glaring. "Do you like him?"

I blink at him. "Why would you think that? I just met him! And I think you should just tell him you're alive." I pick him up and hold him up to my face. In spite of the glow outside, the light is dim under the wagon's canopy.

Kai frowns.

"Why are you afraid? He's your father's most trusted soldier, isn't he?"

"Yes."

"You wouldn't have to sit in my pocket all day."

He sighs and rubs his hand over his eye. "El . . . I have a question first."

I hesitate. "No, I don't like him."

"Not that." He shakes his head and wiggles until I open my hands so he rests in my palm. "When you were at Samuel's place. You said you pushed them away."

I feel my jaw tighten.

"When I . . . arrested your mother . . . I knew you had neighbors who loved you like I did, and I thought someone would step in and help and . . . it was never ever my intention that you would feel so hurt you would push everyone away. It was never my intention for you to be alone."

I'm grateful he's a frog, because I can set him in the bowl and he can't grab me and make me stay. He didn't think I would push everyone away? He didn't think I would be that hurt? I pour some water from the pouch into the bowl with Kai.

He croaks and hops out. "It's freezing!"

"Sorry! I didn't know."

I hear Garrett's boots crunch on the ground before he opens the wagon's door again. "I've got the fire started. What can I help with in here?"

I have leaned on the counter, blocking Kai from his view. "I have a hypothetical question for you."

He raises a single eyebrow and looks me up and down. "Okay."

"Let's say I knew Kai was turned into a frog."

Garrett's brows pinch. "Okay?"

"Before you arrested me."

He doesn't answer, but his lips tighten.

"Because he found me last night seeking help."

"You knew?" Garrett snaps.

"He made me keep it a secret." I straighten, revealing Kai, now sitting at the edge of the bowl.

He raises a frog hand. "Hello, Captain."

Garrett's eyes widen. He doesn't react right away. It's like he didn't believe Kai had actually been turned into a frog so he has to realize that too. "You're . . . serious?" He looks to me for further explanation.

I gesture to Kai. "This is Kai."

"The prince," Kai adds. "And you're flirting with someone I care about."

I glare down at him.

"Says someone who is married," Garrett points out.

"Wait, you can understand him?" I ask.

"Yes." Garrett leans a hand on the doorframe of the wagon.

Kai tilts his head. "Unfortunate."

"Kai." I frown at him, then look up at Garrett. "I wonder if maybe you can understand him because he's not naturally born a frog?" I fold my arms as I ponder on it.

"What really happened the night of your wedding?" Garrett asks carefully.

"The short version of the story," Kai says, "is that Princess Genoa presented me with the golden ball and when I touched it, it turned me into this."

"Why didn't you come to one of us for help? Or your father?" He shakes his head.

Kai shrugs. "I know Elowyn can speak with animals. I didn't know you would be able to understand me too. Not only that, but . . . after it happened, Genoa didn't seem concerned until I started hopping away. It felt wrong. She knew it was going to happen."

"Because she's a fairy," I add. "But apparently no one

can see that she has very obviously pointed ears and enormous wings."

"I don't know," Kai objects for the first time. "I met her a few months ago. Fairies can't be in our world."

Garrett pinches the bridge of his nose. "Wait. All day, no since yesterday . . . you had him this entire time?"

"Who else was going to keep him safe?" I argue.

"Was he in the castle with you this morning?" He shifts his glare to me.

"Yes. He didn't want me to tell anyone."

Garrett runs his fingers through his hair and lets out a heavy breath. "We can't go back and change what happened." He sighs and rests his hands on his hips. "Are you all right, Your Highness?" He looks at Kai.

"Other than being stuck as an amphibian?" He slips into the water. "I'm positively miserable."

I begin gathering the ingredients for dinner again, taking the sweet potato out of the pot. "Then it's a good thing we have a plan to fix you."

Garrett holds out his hands. "Give me a pot and I'll get some water in it. In a wagon, we might not make it until tomorrow night or the next morning. It depends on the weather."

I look up at the clear sky. The rain stopped hours ago, and there isn't a cloud to obscure the giant moon. "Would walking be faster than being burdened with a wagon?"

"Hm?" He pinches his brows as I hand him the pot. "Oh,

no. Horses are faster, but wagons are great because you won't get tired."

"Me?"

"I'm used to being on my feet all day."

I don't let go of the pot as he tries to take it. "And I sit on my throne eating grapes?"

Garrett clears his throat. "Again, that's not what I meant."

"Maybe you should start saying what you mean." I let go of the pot and slam the door of the wagon in his face.

"Do you find him attractive?"

"What?" I spin to face the frog. "Why in the four winds would you say such a thing? Did you not hear any of that?"

"Not all of it is banter, is it?"

I scoff. "Is the married prince jealous?"

"El, that's not—"

"No! You know what, even if I did like him, it's none of your business. You're married now. My love life has nothing to do with you anymore." I snatch the ingredients and hop out of the back of the wagon.

Stabbing things feels like a great activity, because I don't understand my own emotions. My belly is on fire and I want a drink of water. I know deep down I'm jealous Kai is married. Of course I want to fall in love with someone, and I can't have him. Is that someone Garrett? I don't know! He seems to be politely irritated being here.

I peel off the exterior of the sweet potato, then begin

chopping it up, making sure to dice it into small pieces because it's the only outlet I have right now. Some pieces may be a little too small.

"What happened?" Acorn asks through a yawn as he peeks his head from the pouch.

"Nothing," I grumble. "And everything."

"Where is Whiskers?" He looks around.

"Getting water for dinner." I turn to the small onion, which has begun sprouting.

He drops out of the pouch and stretches. "Why are you upset?"

"I'm not!" I sigh and press my palm to my forehead. "Garrett now knows Kai is here and Kai thinks I'm flirting with Garrett."

Acorn smacks his lips and climbs out of the pouch to begin nibbling the peels of the sweet potato. "Are you?"

I frown, but Acorn can't see it. "I met the man this morning. I don't know him. Is he attractive, other than his mustache? Yes. Does it matter? No. Because as soon as Kai is back to being a prince, he'll return to his fairy bride and Garrett will return to the king's side, and I'll go . . . home." I hate how my heart twists. This journey would have been easier without the two men coming along.

"I collected water in the pot and in our drinking pouches. It's nice and clean." Garrett sits down across the fire from me and places the pot on top of a makeshift stand I haven't noticed until now. He's somehow managed to prop up two rocks to support the pot over the flames.

"You must spend a lot of time outside," I say.

He shrugs. "A fair amount. Especially when we're deployed."

"Do you like it?"

He looks up at the starry sky and a genuine smile spreads across his face. "Who couldn't love this?"

I follow his gaze. I don't. I would much rather be in my home, bundled up under my favorite knitted blanket by the fire, drinking a warm cup of tea while reading. But if Kai had said that?

I dump in the ingredients, add a mad dash of salt, and climb to my feet to get my sweater. With the sun gone, it's too cold to pretend I'm not. And maybe I need a moment away from Garrett.

Kai is no longer in the water, and I trace the trail of wet puddles to where he sits at the edge of the counter. "I . . . couldn't get down," he admits softly.

I pull my sweater down over my head and tug out my braid. "I think frog bodies are pretty indestructible. Remember chasing them when we were kids?"

"Of course I do. I remember everything. Elowyn, I still . . . care about you."

I don't reply and pick him up. "It's cold outside. I don't know how warm you'll stay, but we can keep you near the fire. There are a lot of bugs flying around that you can eat."

"Will you please have a conversation with me?"

"There's nothing to say, Kai." I feel weary. "We were best friends and you betrayed me." I step out of the back of the wagon and let the door close.

He huffs. "You keep saying that, but you've never let me share my side of what happened. You run away every time I try. Even now!"

"How can you possibly rationalize what you did to my mother?"

"Don't you get it?" he shouts. "It was her or you! Who was I going to choose?"

I stare down at him. He was forced to choose? "Why didn't you just tell me this?" I ask softly.

"I've tried!" He grabs onto my thumb with both hands. "I've been trying to tell you, but I wasn't sure what good it would do. I didn't want you to believe I was justifying my behavior. What I did was terrible! To both of you! I had to try one last time before I got married. I asked you to let me tell you my side. I said I was sorry. When you wouldn't forgive me, I knew I had to move forward with the wedding. I'm sorry, El. I'm really, terribly sorry for what I did. I didn't want you to be alone. I thought . . . I hoped you would be better without me in your life. I don't know! I messed up."

I look away, remembering that I have an audience.

Garrett is busying himself with stoking the fire and pretending not to eavesdrop, but it's impossible given that we're the only group within probably miles.

I slowly sit on the ground and set Kai on a stone on the

edge of the fire. It's hard to wrap my mind around being so caught up in my own emotions that I wouldn't let Kai explain himself. He approached me at least a dozen times over the year, and I turned him away each time. Once, he tried to hold on to me, saying it was important to listen to him. I yelled at him instead. I don't recall everything I said, but none of it was kind. He looked so hurt when I left. I shouldn't have been so hard on him. I should have forgiven him a long time ago.

I lost him over something he had no choice in.

"Was it your father's command?" I finally bring myself to ask.

"Yes." I wish I could see his human expression. His bulging frog eyes don't show emotion the way they should.

"Why?" My voice is tight. "What does he have against my mother and me?"

Kai leans forward and stretches out so his frog hands are on my knee. "Father was hoping to force you to attend the university, which would get you out of Parshen. He gave me the command to arrest you or your mother shortly after I got home from the war at the edge of Arcoren." His hands begin to slip, so I lift Kai into my hands again. "Father was holding a bundle of letters I had tried to send you. He ranted about how he had explicitly forbidden our friendship, how he wanted to get rid of magic, blah blah. And then he ordered me to arrest you or your mother. I didn't understand why back then, but now . . ." He doesn't finish the sentence. He doesn't need to.

Because his father is evil. King Willard knew his son couldn't be distracted by me if I were in prison, and he had to have known that if he sent Kai to arrest my mother that I would blame Kai. Either way, he would get what he wanted.

Kai and I separated.

I swallow a growing lump in my throat. "Remember how he told you my illiteracy would rub off on you?"

"And he didn't know I was the one teaching you to read?" I can almost see Kai's teasing smile.

A pit grows in my stomach. "I'm sorry." I didn't know that saying those words would bring forth all of the emotions I've buried for the past several months.

I am *not* about to cry in front of these men.

Getting up, I make an excuse that I have to take care of Pancho, practically drop Kai, and manage to keep my composure as I walk around the wagon. I bite my lip hard to hold back a sob threatening to break. When I get around the wagon I find Pancho already unhooked and grazing nearby. I slump against the wagon wheel and slowly fall to my knees, struggling to gulp breaths and keep the tears at bay.

I could have had Kai as a friend this entire time.

I could have had someone to lean on.

We might have been able to work together to come up with a way to get my mother out of prison, or how to get his father to see the good in magic, or . . .

A large hand rests on my shoulder and I tense. "You don't have to be alone anymore," Garrett whispers. He kneels on one knee at my side, letting his hand drop to his knee.

I pull away, wiping the tears off my face. "I'll be fine. I just needed a moment." I don't meet his gaze.

"I know what it's like not to trust others," he says comfortingly. "Once you find where you belong, you'll realize that it's okay to let people in. You just need to find where you belong."

"I really don't need advice right now." I don't accept his hand when I go to stand, choosing to pull myself up using the wagon wheel instead.

"Elowyn!" Acorn screams. "An owl just stole Kai!"

# Chapter Ten

Chasing an owl through the woods—an owl carrying the prince of the land—isn't how I imagined my first night camping in the woods going. Luckily for us, Kai is yelling at me the entire time:

"You didn't warn me about owls!"

"It's going to drop me and I'm going to die!"

"Elowyn, if I don't make it out of this, I always loved you!"

"El, I'm going to kill you!"

I wish I had time to dwell on the fact that he loves me. It's not like I didn't have a feeling he did, or that I've entertained the same feelings, I just never thought he would admit it.

Unfortunately, the owl isn't deterred by Kai's shouts, and if it weren't for his noise, I would never be able to follow the otherwise silent owl.

"Keep yelling!" I shout up to Kai.

"What happens if it eats me? Ah!"

Unfortunately, the brightness of the moon doesn't pierce through the tree leaves, and I'm running practically blind. I've also got my attention focused on the shadow I catch now and then, which means I am not paying attention to where I'm going. I trip and fall, landing hard on my hands and knees. I hiss as my left hand gets torn up on something thorny, but I pick myself up and continue running.

"I am really tired of being a frog!" Kai shouts in desperation. His voice has turned to my right and it's getting further away.

I shift direction. "Little owl!" I plead. "Wait! You have my friend!" I don't realize I've run through a bush until it tears at my skirts and catches the toe of my left boot. I let out a shout of shock as I tumble down an unseen steep and stony incline. My ribs explode in agony and white flashes through my vision. "Slugs of the earth!" I lie on the ground a moment when I stop rolling, arms and legs sprawled.

"That was graceful," a light voice floats down from above.

I tilt my chin up and see the owl resting on a branch in the tree I'm now looking up into. Her golden eyes reflect the moonlight in a shocking bright yellow.

I slowly sit up. "That frog isn't dinner. He's my friend."

The owl clutches Kai in one taloned foot. His poor little frog body bulges above and below the foot as he's squeezed. She turns her head and blinks large eyes. "Frogs are food." She hoots as if to make a point.

I stand and clutch my ribs. "Not that one. He's the prince." I don't even know if owls have a clue what a prince is, so I shake my head. "He's important to me. He's mine."

"I caught it."

Knowing owls are also sometimes predators of opportunity, it does me no good to say I caught him first. I'm lost for words and I can hardly breathe. "I can help you catch something else."

"Mine." It pecks at the top of Kai's head, making him scream.

Garrett shows up, holding up a chunk of raw pinkish meat in his hand like it's a torch. "I've got something better!"

The owl tilts its head. It blinks. Looks at Kai. And then drops him to swoop down and get the meat from Garrett, who apparently brought it with him.

"Help!" Kai shouts as he drops.

I run and fall on my stomach, sliding with my arms outstretched to catch him before he hits the ground. He lands in my hands and I close them around him. "Gotcha!" I pant and look over my shoulder. "Is it gone?"

Garrett is wiping his hand on his pant leg, looking into the darkness. "Think so."

I groan as I sit up. It takes three gasps for me to fully get up to my knees and open my hands.

Kai stares at me, breathing hard.

I feel my lips tugging.

He closes his mouth.

I burst into laughter. After a moment or two, Garrett breaks into a smile before he joins me in laughter, resting his hands on his knees as he doubles over.

Kai doesn't laugh at first. "I nearly died."

"Oh, that's going to be a funny story to share with your family," I say.

"*You* fell down a cliff," he counters. But either from relief or because he finally sees the humor in the situation, Kai releases a chuckle.

I push myself up to my feet. I must look ridiculous, covered in twigs, leaves, and whatever else the forest bestowed on me when I fell down the hill. "How do we find our way back?"

"Considering you fell *down* a hill, I recommend climbing back up it," Kai suggests.

I roll my eyes. "That much is obvious."

"It's a pretty steep hill, the way you came," Garrett says. "I recommend going around it." He points his thumb over his shoulder. "The way I came."

I hear Kai huff.

"Winds, are you jealous?" I whisper to him.

"Clam up."

I grin and walk to Garrett and then gasp. "I completely left Acorn on his own!" Worry grips my chest.

"Acorn is in the wagon," Garrett says. He turns and begins leading the way he came from. "I put him in there when I got the meat. I don't think he was very happy about it because he was screeching like I was killing him."

I can't help but smile because I can very much imagine

Acorn yelling that he wanted to come and didn't want to be left behind. "Thank you for making sure he was safe."

"We wouldn't have found that owl if you couldn't speak with it." Garrett glances over his shoulder at me.

"You couldn't hear Kai waking up the entire forest?"

"I wasn't waking up the entire forest" he objects. "And even if I was, good! How else would you have chased down the owl?"

"I wouldn't have." I tighten my hands around him and pull him closer to my body. "That thought crossed my mind."

"Careful with this log." Garrett steps over something large and black.

"How can you see anything?" I step over the log after Garrett.

He speaks over his shoulder. "My eyes have adjusted to the darkness. Have yours not?"

I glance around. "I can make out basic shapes, but I don't exactly spend time running through the woods at night."

"You don't? It's my favorite pastime."

"He's joking," Kai explains from my hands.

I resist the urge to roll my eyes. "I gathered that. I'm not entirely dense, you know."

"It's a soldier thing," Kai expands. "We do a lot of tracking at night while the enemy sleeps."

"Oh. That actually makes sense." I watch the back of

Garrett and notice he's holding his cloak over his arm so it won't snag on anything, which gives me the perfect view of his back. And backside. Which I notice only when he begins climbing over a large stone.

I pause on the other side and blink.

He holds out his hand. "What?"

"You couldn't go around it?"

"I suppose I could have, but the path is right here."

I raise a brow.

"There's a cliff to your left. Want to try that instead?" He nudges his head.

I look to my left, which appears to be adorned with bushes . . . until it dawns on me that those are actually tree tops, and to my left is actually a ravine. "I didn't realize we went up and down . . ."

"Can I help you over the boulder now?"

I reluctantly accept his hand. "Only because I have Kai and can't grip the rock like I want to." I feel the need to explain this because I am *not* holding his hand.

"Mm-hm."

I take his hand. It's warm and rough from constant use, and it completely envelops mine. He holds just tightly enough to offer me support, but there is gentleness in his grip. When I land on the other side, Garrett lets go and I find my heart drop with his hand.

The dying campfire comes into view, then the shape of the wagon, and my momentary disappointment is replaced with relief.

I grimace and rub my side, my ribs starting to ache as my adrenaline ebbs. "Dinner is going to be mushy."

"Well, at least it will be done." Garrett glances over his shoulder at me. "I'm sure it will taste fine."

"Elowyn, is that you?" I hear Acorn's voice yell from the back of the wagon.

"Yes! And we have Kai."

"And you left me out of it! Why don't I get to go on adventures?"

"What do you think we're on right now?" I go to the wagon and open the back door.

Acorn scrunches his face at me. "This is a boring adventure."

"Not to me," Kai counters.

I hold my hand out to Acorn. "Let's get out some of those caterpillars for you both to eat. I imagine Kai isn't feeling up to trying to catch flies right now."

"I'm not feeling like caterpillars either, but here we are."

I return to the fire and set the two animals down. Garrett has removed the pot from the fire and stoked it back into a warm glow. With the light, I can now assess Kai's head where the owl poked it, and there's luckily only a tiny cut. To him, it probably hurts terribly.

"Garett, will you keep an eye on him while I get some poultice?"

He nods, but Acorn stands beside Kai and makes his

prickles stand out.

I return to the wagon to get the ointment. My ribs pang with pain as I pull myself into it, and then scoop out a tiny bit of the ointment with the back of my fingernail to carefully apply it to Kai's bare amphibian head.

"That should help." I screw the lid back on. "It will take away the pain and you'll be nice and scabbed by morning. Maybe even healed."

"You make the best poultice."

"You're welcome." I turn my attention to Garrett.

He lifts up a bowl. "Ready to eat? It's not bad. Little mushy like we expected, but it tastes great."

"Good." I accept the second bowl and take a bite. The flavor is there, but the texture makes me gag. "How can you eat this?"

Garrett spoons another mouthful. "I'm not picky. Good food is good food."

I shake my head. With nothing else to eat, I'm going to have to suck it up too. When I look down at Acorn handing Kai a caterpillar, I realize things could be much, *much* worse.

Garrett finishes and stands. "I'll go rinse out the dishes in the river."

"I brought blankets. The wagon is a little tight, but if—"

"I have a bedroll. You sleep in there." He accepts my bowl and nods to me. "Good night, Elowyn."

"Th-thanks," I stammer.

"Your hand is bleeding," Acorn points out.

I look down at the palm of my left hand. It's already scabbed. "I'll be fine. It mostly stings. I must have landed on a thorn bush." I carry the two of them into the wagon and can't help but look back at Garrett as he disappears into the trees.

"At least he's pulling his weight," Kai comments.

"Mm." I close the door, set them down on the counter, and remove my boots. "It's cold out there. Will he be warm enough, Kai?"

"He's an experienced soldier. I promise he's been in much colder weather. If he's worth half his salt, he has a good bedroll and blanket and will be plenty warm."

"He's got the fire too!" Acorn chimes in. "But if you want, I can keep his toes warm."

I don't miss Acorn's mischievous smile or how he bristles, and I giggle. "I'm positive he would love sleeping with your poking warmth."

After setting the blankets on the floor of the wagon, I pull my hair from its braid, letting my long black hair cascade down. It gives me a chance to massage my aching scalp and pull out the leaves and twigs that have lodged themselves in my hair. My hands freeze, my eyes widen, and my stomach drops. "My hat!"

I throw the door open and jump out.

Garrett is in his bedroll and props himself up on an elbow. He's draped his cloak on top of his bedroll as a second blanket. "What is it?"

I can't see it anywhere. It is the only gift I still have from my mother, other than my pathetic grimoire. "My hat," I repeat. To anyone else, it might be a simple inconvenience to replace a hat. But it's not something I can so easily replace.

The camping area shows no trace.

"I must have lost it when I fell," I say. I bite my bottom lip and awkwardly face Garrett, then flash a smile. I hope he can't see my sadness behind it. "It's not . . . a big deal." I swallow the lump in my throat. "I have an extra blanket." I point my thumb at the wagon before awkwardly turning to get one of them for him.

He is out of his bedroll by the time I get back and accepts it. "Thank you." He offers a smile.

I tuck my hair behind my ear. "Good night."

I don't know why I feel embarrassed as I return to the wagon and close the door. He's not even that attractive! And yet, I can't help but think about the confusing politeness and relentless teasing I've experienced all day with him, or the way my frog prince got so bothered by it. I feel the blanket being tugged up closer to my chin and the brush of a cold touch on my cheek as I finally drift into sleep.

## Chapter Eleven

I wake to the sound of dripping and bolt upright in a panic that my sink is leaking and probably has been all night—or worse, that the window is leaking again and I'm going to need to get some help sealing it shut. However, when I sit upright, a blast of pain explodes through my ribs and I am mildly confused to find myself bundled up in the back of my wagon. And then I remember everything all at once: Kai, Garrett, the journey, the owl.

"Let me see your ribs." It's Kai's voice, but when I look around, he's still just a frog and sits to my left on a shelf of washcloths.

I rub my side. "It can't be that bad. I probably just hit them on a stone when I fell down the hill."

"You fell down a hill?" Acorn scampers across the counter to gaze down at me. "And I didn't get to see it?"

"Aren't you glad I left you here? You could have been squashed if you were in the pouch with me," I point out.

He pouts. "True."

I sigh and lift my under dress, making sure to keep the blanket across my waist, and pull it up to expose my skin to the bitter morning air. I shudder against the cold, which makes me gasp instantly. The light in the wagon is dim, and it takes me a moment to make out the discoloration on my side.

"Where is the poultice?" Kai hops off the shelf onto my knee, turns, and hops up to the counter. He's gaining more confidence as a frog.

"It's not that big of a deal," I try to object, but Acorn helps him find it. A low rumble echoes across the sky and I gasp. "Garrett! He's been out in the rain." I roll to my knees to get to my feet.

"I'm not wet," I hear from under the wagon.

I tilt my head, but the slats of wood are covered in my blankets, and I don't think there would be a hole big enough to see through it anyway. "You slept under the wagon?"

"Only when it started raining." I hear him groan and the shuffle of fabric. "I'm going to get wet getting out, though."

"He can just stay there," Kai mutters.

I lean back on my heels. "I suppose this means no fire. How badly is it raining?"

"It's a light drizzle, but it's been raining for hours so everything is wet," he responds. "Too wet for a fire, but I have enough for a cold breakfast for us both. I've got a couple of blueberry orange biscuits, and nuts we can share. I've got salted beef for myself too. It should be more than enough until lunch."

Kai croaks and pushes the poultice jar closer to me.

"I have a jar of canned peaches too," I offer.

"I love peaches."

It makes me smile. I open the poultice, dip my fingers into the chilly ointment, and rub it over my ribs. Touching them hurts far worse than I anticipated, and I let out a hiss between my teeth.

"Everything okay?" Garrett asks.

"I got bruised last night falling down the hill." I look down at my ribs again. The sun is finally waking and offers a bit more light than moments ago, and I know this bruise is just going to spread. Sitting on a tilting wagon all day is going to be miserable.

"Don't forget your hand," Kai coaxes.

I drop my shirt. "I was going to do that next. Though, it's rather inconvenient. I need to use this hand to get breakfast ready."

"I can help," Kai insists.

Acorn snorts. "How? By getting frog skin on everything?"

"My skin isn't spreading everywhere," he counters.

"Your frog juices are."

"That's water!"

My lips pinch, resisting a smile. I never thought I would hear Kai arguing with Acorn, and it makes me happy to hear them.

"Are you sure it's not pee?" Acorn adds. "Did you pee?"

Kai croaks, though I believe he meant to growl. He's hardly threatening. "It's a good thing you're the prickly one."

"You two," I chuckle as I climb to my feet.

"Is Prince Kaison arguing with Acorn?" Garrett asks from beneath the wagon. I can hear things shuffling and imagine he's putting his bedding away.

"I wish you could understand Acorn too," I say. "It's rather amusing." I pull my dress back on, wool stockings, and boots before I get my sweater.

And then I freeze.

Because sitting on the floor near the back door of the wagon is my hat. I lift it up and run my thumb over the brim. Garrett went back and found it? Why would he do that?

"Mind if I come in?" Garrett says from the back of the wagon.

"Go ahead." I put on the hat. "You'll be at least a little warmer in here."

He opens the door and I catch a glimpse of the wet landscape behind him. A fine mist hovers in the trees and a gust of cold air fills the wagon. He closes the door and slips his muddy boots off. "I've got Pancho hooked up again. I think we should be able to make it to the waterfall today, as long as the roads aren't too muddy, or the wagon might get stuck." He runs his fingers through his hair. The back of the right side is sticking up. He's not wearing his cloak, but has it draped over his arm, and his shirt is a bit disheveled.

"You got my hat."

He smiles. "You were upset it was lost. It wasn't hard to

find."

"But . . . you took the time to do it." I want to tell him that Kai's the only other person to do nice things like this for me.

Garrett shrugs. "It wasn't a problem." He sits on the floor and rummages through his pack, removing bundles of things wrapped in brown paper I assume to be the food for breakfast.

I pass a nut to Acorn. "Are you getting enough to eat, Kai?"

He croaks and his shoulders lift in a shrug. "I am hungry. I suppose with it being muddy outside I should go look for some worms." He looks toward the back door.

"Acorn can go with you," I suggest.

"No way am I getting muddy when I can stay nice and warm in here." Acorn heads for his bed.

I pick him up. "Kai can't dig. You can."

He bristles, but I've handled him long enough his spikes are only uncomfortable.

"Please?"

"I can manage." Kai leaps off the counter, landing on top of Garrett's head.

Garrett cringes and visibly resists the urge to grab Kai.

Kai drops down to his shoulder and then to the ground. "Thank you, Captain." One more hop and he's at the back door.

Garrett's lips tighten. "No problem."

I step over Garrett. "Give me a moment to put on my boots and I'll go with you." I scoop Kai up in my free hand before he can jump out and sit myself on the edge of the floor so I can bend down and set both Kai and Acorn in the mud. I have to hold my breath doing so as pain burns up and down my right side.

"I'm sure they can manage," Garrett says. "Birds shouldn't be out hunting in this weather."

"They could be. It's barely raining." I bite my bottom lip and grunt—or whine—in pain while I try to tug on my boots. I place my hands on the floorboards to push off, but Garrett snatches my wrist before I can.

He frowns and lifts my arm, making me wince. His blue eyes darken a little further and he pulls my shirt and bodice up to expose my ribs.

"Garrett! Stop it!" But when I actually see my ribs in full light, I realize just how bad the bruising is.

He breathes out my name. "Elowyn! Does it hurt to breathe?"

I pull away and push my shirt down. "Of course it does." I slide out of the wagon.

He stares at me, mouth agape, then comes to and slips his boots back on before following me. "Let me keep an eye on them. You need to rest. Did you bring bandages?"

"Can ribs be bound?" I wrap my arms around myself. It's not cold enough to see our breath, but I still shiver, which does nothing to help.

Acorn scurries toward the base of a sagebrush bush, muttering about finding worms quickly so he can go to sleep.

Kai doesn't follow, but watches me.

"Of course they can. And you should." Garrett steps up to my side. "If you move too much, and your ribs really are broken, you could puncture your lung or something else."

"Why do you care?" I turn my head to look up at him.

He frowns and takes a little too long to answer. "It's my duty to keep you alive."

"Am I dying?"

"Not yet." He folds his arms across his chest.

I pat his arm. "Then stop worrying about me."

"Kai, get over here!" Acorn shouts at him.

Kai hops once, looks back, and then hops the rest of the way to Acorn.

Garrett shakes his head and returns to the wagon. "Let me know when you're ready to go."

Acorn digs at the base and tugs out worms, giving them to Kai and eating a few himself. "Fresh worms after a rain are actually much more delicious. Sometimes you can even break into logs and get some termites to munch. Well, I can. It's sort of fun having someone to scavenge around with. Ellie! Can we get a frog after Kai is a human again?"

I return to them and chuckle. "I suppose we can look into that. Unless Kai wants to just stay as our pet."

"Oh, that is a lovely idea!" Acorn spins to face Kai. "Do

you want to?"

"No. Not at all." He gulps down the last worm. "Should we take some with us?"

Acorn sniffs around toward another bush. "I think we should. The caterpillars won't last past today."

After assisting in the collection of possibly a dozen or so worms, I return to the wagon to find that Garrett has folded all of my blankets and stored them away and now has his cloak on again.

He extends a bundle, which I assume is my breakfast. "Are you ready?" He glances at my muddy hands. "You are . . . not like any woman I have ever met. I saw an empty . . ." He crouches. "Ah. Here." He lifts up a jar and unscrews the lid so I can dump the worms inside. "Do you want to rinse your hands so you can eat your breakfast? I can show you to the river."

"I can do it." I dust my hands on my skirt and head away to find the river. It will give me a chance to relieve myself too.

"Don't look at her like that," I hear Kai say.

I can't decide if I hear Garrett say "You had a chance" or "You lost your chance," or maybe it's none of those and he just said, "Look at her pants," but when I glance over my shoulder all three of them are watching me. I roll my eyes and hurry to rinse off and return to the wagon.

The day is arduous and slow, but the rain stops shortly after breakfast. My ribs continue to ache, though the poultice helps each time I apply it.

"This must be the toll bridge," I say as Pancho comes to a stop.

The wooden bridge dangles over a gorge about eighteen feet deep. It seems to be in good shape, as the ropes aren't frayed and the planks aren't rotting or broken.

Garrett drops down from the wagon and walks around the tree at the edge of the bridge to see around it. "There isn't anywhere to pay." He pauses and turns in a circle before returning. "I don't see a hut for shelter either. I didn't know this was a toll bridge."

"I wouldn't know either way. Let's go, Pancho."

The wagon rumbles forward, and a hollow rhythm sounds beneath the donkey's hooves and the wagon wheels. The ropes groan as they tighten with our weight.

"I would almost rather walk at this point," I mutter, rubbing my ribs.

"Did you apply more poultice, like I told you to?" Garrett asks, side-eyeing me.

I roll my eyes. "Of course I did. I've applied it three times today."

He points his thumb over his shoulder. "You must have an oral pain killer back there. You should take some."

"Why are you worrying about this? I'm fine."

"You're uncomfortable. That isn't fine." His blue eyes are earnest.

"No, but you can't heal it and neither can I. Stop treating

me like a child."

He sighs. "I'm sorry. I'm not trying to. I only want to—"

The bridge tilts sharply to the left and I yell out in shock as I am nearly thrown out of the wagon. Garrett reaches his arm out across my body and places it on my hip. I cling to his arm out of sheer desperation not to slide off.

A booming voice echoes through the ravine below. "Who is this crossing my bridge?"

An enormous green face appears with eyes as big as the wagon wheels, a nose wide and flat, and when it licks its fat lips, I can see rotting teeth inside.

I gasp. "Samuel didn't mean toll bridge. He meant *troll* bridge!"

# Chapter Twelve

The wagon slides toward the troll's massive hand, but one of the wheels catches on a broken plank. The jolt ripples and dislodges me from Garrett's hold. Luckily, I'm still clinging to him and my grip tightens when my legs slip from the wagon so I'm hanging in the air.

"Don't you dare let go!" I shout at him.

His right hand holds to the side of the wagon, keeping both of us on. "I'm trying not to," he says through gritted teeth. He shifts his grip onto my forearm, holding as tightly as possible. The muscles in his arms are taut with effort.

My ribs explode in agony as I'm pulled with my arms over my head.

Garrett's blue eyes snap to the troll. "My name is Captain Garrett Bath of the king's guard! I command you to release us immediately as you are impeding the mission we have been given from King Willard the Seventh, which requires us to cross this bridge!"

"King's guard?" The troll leans closer. The ropes groan in protest and I know if he puts any more pressure on them, they'll snap. His rancid breath floats over us.

I hold my breath as tears sting my eyes. My grip is

slipping.

"I never eaten one of them. You look like your hide is tough. But juicy." A ball of drool plops down on the bridge to my left.

Pancho is scrambling to stay on the bridge. "Help! Elowyn! Help! Falling!" His hooves clatter loudly.

Things inside the wagon are dislodging and falling against the canopy, and I hope Acorn and Kai have found a place to stay safe.

"Please don't eat us!" I beg. "Let us cross! We can find something else for you to eat!"

"You've got a nice donkey there. I like donkey." The troll lifts his hand off the bridge, which snaps it back into place and makes it sway.

My legs land hard against the edge of the bench, but I scramble back on and wrap my arms around Garrett for a better grip in case the troll tips the bridge again. Garrett wraps his arm around my shoulders and grabs a fistful of the side of my skirt and bodice top in a more secure hold.

Pancho screams as the troll picks him up and breaks the arms of the wagon away.

"No!" I yell. "Don't eat him! Please! We need him!"

I wish I knew more magic, more that would be useful in a situation like this. I can't cast a fireball or lightning storm like the sorcerers can, and I can't make a windstorm out of nowhere.

But I know potions.

"Let go." I push against Garrett.

He hesitates before listening, and I scramble into the back of the wagon.

It's an absolute disaster. Potions and vials are mixed with broken fruit preserves. I rummage through the jars, looking for the vial of glittering orange liquid I know I brought with me. I can't immediately see Kai or Acorn, but I have no time to search for them either. Finally, I spot the vial wedged under the bench and snatch it up. But another vial catches my eye. A blue one. If I time this right, I could save us.

I scramble back over the bench.

Garrett grabs my legs to steady me. "Careful!"

The troll tilts his head back and dangles Pancho over his mouth. He seems to be enjoying the terror in Pancho's body as he yells to me for help.

With all the strength I have, I throw the orange vial, and cry out as soon as I do so. I fall to my knee on the bench, gasping and clutching my side. Garrett pulls me against him.

The vial strikes the troll right in the eye and explodes. A puff of orange mist floats around his head and he sucks in a big breath. And then another. He drops his hand down on the opposite cliff wall, unintentionally releasing Pancho, and lets out a loud sneeze that makes the world around us tremble.

"What was that? Please say it's something to kill him."

"I don't . . . kill people," I say through gritted teeth.

"Then what was it?"

I watch the troll. "It's a joke potion. Sneezing. I sell them to the kids. I hoped to distract him. I need . . . him closer." I squeeze my eyes shut in pain.

I don't have the strength to push Garrett away. It hurts to breathe. I barely even care that Garrett has lifted me into his arms and slipped off the wagon's bench. I would prefer he were Kai, but he's not, and I don't know what to do about this new realization.

The troll wrinkles his nose, a glob of snot hanging from his right nostril. "What was that?" He sneezes again. "Because of you, I've lost my lunch!"

"If you do not stop, I will have no choice but to act in defense of the throne," Garrett says with authority dripping from his tone. It would probably look better if he were holding his sword instead of me, but he's taking deliberate steps toward the opposite side of the ravine.

"Aye? What are you gonna do? Poke me with your little stick?" He leans his face close. "I'll give you the first strike for free."

Garrett stops. He glances at me, at the other side of the ravine, and back at the troll, clearly contemplating his options.

"Put me down." I show him the blue vial.

His eyes narrow in a way that asks if I'm positive he should do that.

I nod.

"Okay." Garrett slowly rests me on my feet.

I turn to the troll and use my thumb to pop the cork from the mouth of the bottle as I approach him. "You are intelligent. You must let *some* people pass. What do you ask in return?"

He snorts, sending the snot raining down.

Garrett quickly steps between me and the troll so he is shielding me, and the snot hits him on the back. "Eww." His shoulders rise to his ears.

"You want to barter?" The troll laughs.

Garrett frowns. "I have to fight him. It's the only way," he whispers. "You don't need to watch this. Go back and find Prince Kaison and Acorn."

"Garrett, give me a chance." I grab his arm. I know he's a soldier. I know he knows how to fight. But has he ever taken on a troll by himself? I doubt it.

He pushes me away and draws his sword.

The troll grins and leans his head over the bridge so he's feet from us. "One strike, human."

With all the strength I have left, I throw the blue vial into the troll's face. Kai taught me how to throw stones, a talent I used to scare off wolves a couple of winters ago. My aim is right on, and it lands in the troll's mouth.

He coughs and splutters, his brows knitting in confusion. His eyes momentarily widen. He scratches at his throat. And then his hands begin to shrink. His arms are next. Then his head, legs, and finally torso.

I lean over the side of the bridge.

The troll, once several men tall, is now barely the size of Garrett.

Garrett appears by my side.

"What just happened?" Garrett mutters.

"Shrinking potion. It's a rather useful enchantment too." I smile in relief. "We need to go, though. I don't know how long he'll stay small—it isn't an exact science. Yet." I turn away. "Kai! Acorn!"

"We're safe!" a muffled voice shouts back. It's Acorn's.

"I can carry you," Garrett offers.

"I'll be fine," I object. "I'm just slower."

We make it to the wagon, but the tongue has been snapped off and Pancho is nowhere to be seen. My heart aches at the thought. He was a good donkey and hasn't been out in the wild like this. I hope he can find his way home.

"I don't think either of us can move this," Garrett says, studying the wagon. "Let's unload as much of the provisions as we can salvage. I've got enough room in my pack I can carry your bedding. I don't suppose you can make an enchantment for a pack to be bottomless?" He says it in a teasing tone, hoisting his bag out of the mess and resting it on the dislodged side of the wagon.

"I've done it before," I say. "It will hold more than usual, but it won't be bottomless. If we enchant your bag, we have a better chance of it being deeper than mine." I step over to him and grab the strap of the bag. "*Et unding atan.*"

The orb in my pouch grows warm and the bag sparks.

Garrett jumps back, nearly dropping the bag.

A burned smell fills the air and I can't help but grimace, fearing I spoke the incantation incorrectly.

Garrett hesitantly reaches his arm in and his eyes widen when he's able to dip in until the entirety of his arm is inside. "That's incredible. You look shocked," he comments.

"I've never enchanted something to be that deep." I blink.

Garrett shrugs and begins by packing medicines followed by food, which all somehow fits.

My fingers brush the orb in my pouch. Did the ball do something to my spell?

"How far do you think you can walk?" Garrett shoulders his pack, now bulging with everything we may need.

"I think we should go until I physically can't." I settle Acorn in his pouch and hold Kai in my hand.

"If you lean on me as we walk, you may be able to go farther," Garrett offers.

"We'll see." I'm silently hoping the Mirror Falls hold up to their namesake, because I can't live with this pain while trying to negotiate with fairies over Kai's fate. "When we find the fairy ring, are we planning on stepping in and hoping they'll help us? Because if fairies were banished and locked away, wouldn't there be some animosity?"

"They would only have themselves to blame. They

betrayed the king and broke a deal. The consequence was them being banished."

"It's a little of both," Kai says.

I part my hands so I can see him.

He croaks. "My mother couldn't have children. Father got every sorcerer and sorceress and witch and—*croak*—whomever else he could find with magic to help. *Croak.* But nothing they did could grant her children. Until—*croak*—a fairy sorceress showed up and—*croak*—granted her the ability to have children."

My chest tightens. Kai has croaked before, but . . . not while talking. I glance at Garrett to see if he's noticed, and Garrett meets my eyes in a way that tells me he has.

Kai continues as if nothing strange is happening. "The fairies—*croak*—tried to steal me as a baby. *Croak.* So Father locked them away."

I'm not so concerned about what happened with the fairies any longer. "I have the ball. I can offer to return it in exchange for them fixing him," I suggest to Garrett. "It must be valuable. Kai!"

He leaps out of my hands and extends his tongue to catch a small moth and lands on the ground effortlessly. He gulps down the moth, the powder of its wings flecking onto his face.

"Elowyn . . . I think we need to move a little more quickly," Garrett says in a gentle tone.

I feel on edge as my own hands begin to tremble with

worry. "I agree." I quicken my pace, wishing more than ever I had a stronger medicine for broken ribs. That is going to be on my list as soon as I get home.

Kai turns his frog body to face me. "Why are you so frantic? I was hungry."

I force a smile. "I'm not frantic. I need to eat too, and we need to get moving."

Kai ribbits and rubs his frog hand across his face to wipe away the powder. He scrambles up my arm and rests on my shoulder.

Garrett steps up to my side and slides his hand over mine. "We're almost there."

"What if they can't save him?" My voice is tight. "Or what if they refuse? I've lost everyone else. I thought I lost him when he got married, but this is . . ." I swallow hard and look up at the soldier. "This is permanent. I can't even see him again if he's a frog. I can't look into . . ." I catch myself and clear my throat.

Garrett smiles softly and drops his hand. "You must care for him a lot."

I sigh heavily. "Yes. And no. It's complicated," I admit.

"Hm. It doesn't stop the hurt though."

"No." As a child, I insisted I would marry him. As we grew older and he started spending more time in the castle for lessons, he spent less time with me. He was always brilliant, but he is ages ahead of me in knowledge. He also spent more time with higher-class people, and I often watched from a distance. He interacted with proper ladies much differently than he did with me. A part of me realized some time ago that we would never really get married. But it still felt good to pretend.

Garrett expertly changes the subject. "You say you believe the princess is a fairy?"

I give an annoyed sigh.

"I was just thinking about what her motivation would be in marrying Prince Kaison," Garrett explains.

I shake my head. "Not that so much as turning him into a frog. Marrying into the throne makes sense. When the king dies, his son takes . . . over . . ." I blink. "And turning the prince into a frog means *she* can take over the kingdom."

"Huh." Garrett's brows knit together as he works through his own thought process. "It sort of makes sense."

"It's the *only* thing that makes any sense."

Unlike yesterday, the sun is high in the sky and has brought the touch of summer heat with it. I remove my sweater and tuck it so it hangs over the strap of my pouch. In the distance, I can finally hear the roar of the waterfall. We stop for a few minutes in the shade of a tree to take a drink.

"Your mustache is crooked and driving me crazy." I reach out and twist the tip of the left side of his mustache, which has been hanging down all afternoon. Finally, I get it to stay. "You really need to cut this off if you can't at least make it look the same." When I look up into his eyes I feel a pull at my heart.

He reaches up and straightens my hat. "Then you should know how to make your hat straight."

My heart skips. "I don't have a mirror."

"Neither do I."

"I thought with how dashing you always look, you must keep one in your breast pocket." I twitch my brows.

He chuckles and pats his chest. "No breast pocket."

He's close enough I can smell the little bit of scent lingering on his clothes—unless he packed his cologne with him, which I doubt. His eyes are a stunning sky blue with bursts of icy highlights. I could get lost in those eyes.

And then a frog lands on the side of his face.

"Ah!" Garrett grabs Kai and throws him down.

"Garrett!" I scold and scoop up Kai. "Are you all right? What were you thinking?"

"Do I really have to explain?" He might be glaring, but it's hard to tell.

I roll my eyes, because why would he be jealous, and decide to change the subject. "How much longer do you think we have?" I ask Garrett as we start walking again.

"Just a couple of hours. How is your side?"

"It hurts," I confess. "But I'll make it."

The hill the waterfall belongs to looks like a wart in an otherwise flat landscape. I don't know what other roads meet up with this one, but people come into view along the way. Each of them has some sort of ailment—an arm in a sling, burn scars, limping on a cane, riding in a wagon, elderly and arthritic, or unseen illnesses. I should have packed an empty jar so I could collect water, but the best I have might be a small potion bottle.

The road bends around the trees and then suddenly opens, exposing the enormous cliff with the most stunning white waterfall I have ever seen in my life. As it hits the river below it leaves a lovely mist. Vibrant green moss covers the stone nearest the waterfall from top to bottom, and ferns with large leaves dangle between the cracks in the stone. It's like a different part of the world has been ripped from somewhere and deposited here. The foliage looks like nothing I've ever seen.

"This way," Garrett says, beginning the walk around the waterfall.

But there's a cluster of water lilies I *must* investigate. They aren't new to me—we have water lilies in the ponds in the woods, but those are white. These are the most vibrant shade of purple I have ever seen. The yellow centers almost glow. Plump honey bees gather their pollen and distribute it to other flowers as they fly about, creating a magical atmosphere. It's no wonder people believe this water is magical.

"Elowyn?" Garrett calls.

"Coming." Or I was—until Kai leaps from my pocket and onto one of the lily pads. "Kai!" I lunge forward and snatch him with both hands.

And slip right into the water.

I surface and scramble onto the banks, now soaked. Even with the summer heat in the air, the water is freezing and a shiver bursts through me, causing pain to burn through my ribs. I clutch my side and gasp, but the burning slowly fades.

Frog Kai rests near my hand, his throat moving as he stares at me.

"That wasn't funny." I pick up Kai.

"It was." He croaks. "You're all wet now."

I grab my hat floating at the edge of the water, and in doing so, realize my ribs pull but don't explode with the pain they had only moments ago.

"Are you all right, dear?" A woman with two men and a cluster of other women keeps a safe distance as she asks.

"Just wet. I'm fine." I smile and stand.

"You were . . . talking to yourself. Maybe you need another bath in the waters?" She gestures back to the river.

"Oh. No. It's . . ." I hold up the frog and realize that saying I can speak with animals isn't going to stop her from thinking there is something off with me.

Garrett reappears and says nothing as he puts his hand on my back and guides me away from the staring crowd. "Did you pack any extra clothes in my bag?"

"I didn't think I would need them."

Acorn screeches as he clambers out of the dripping pouch. "I'm soaking wet!"

"What were you thinking?" Garrett catches the grumpy hedgehog.

"Kai jumped in." I have my hands close to my body and move my fingers to look down at him.

"The water felt good," Kai explains.

"He must have been dehydrated," I explain. "But it helped my ribs."

Garrett looks between us. "Elowyn, did he just speak?"

I nod slowly.

"I . . . only heard a croak."

I stop dead in my tracks, my breath stolen. "You can't understand him anymore?"

Garrett shakes his head.

"Kai." My chest clenches. I look back at the frog.

Acorn gasps. "Hurry! Kiss him!"

I look at him. "How would that help?"

"True love's kiss! Haven't you heard fairytales?"

I don't care how foolish I look. If it is supposed to work, it's worth a try. I bring the frog to my lips and kiss Kai.

He croaks.

I hold my breath.

Garrett clears his throat. "We're gaining an audience. Come on." He reaches a hand down to help me to my feet.

My heart sinks like a stone. Kai doesn't change.

I've never felt so helpless. I walk as fast as I can with Garrett, away from the riverbanks and further into the woods. We don't say anything because all I can think about is how I have no idea how to help Kai, he's becoming more of a frog, and I'm about to lose him.

Lose him.

It was different "losing him" to a princess when he would still be alive and . . . human. But to lose him to becoming a frog for the rest of his life is far more tragic. I can't walk fast in my soaking skirt, so I stop and pull it off, as well as the top, leaving me in only the beige under dress and the undergarments beneath.

"Elowyn, what are you doing?" Garrett looks around uncomfortably.

"We need to hurry and I'm weighed down by my dress." I throw my hair back in a quick ponytail, set my dripping hat on my dress, and swallow hard. I have to leave it behind. This is for Kai. Material things mean nothing with Kai's life at risk.

I begin up the path Garrett started up. It's little more than a game trail and only visible through the long grass because we are on it.

Garrett follows directly behind me. "Do you want my cloak?" he offers.

"I'm fine." I don't even look back at him.

We have to scramble up rocks in one section in order to shimmy around to the side Samuel mentioned. I'm actually grateful Kai jumped into the water because my ribs feel immensely better, meaning the water from the falls does have healing properties after all. I'll have to return and collect some.

"Watch that rock, it's loose. No, that one." Garrett grabs my leg and moves it so my foot is on a different rock. "There."

I mutter a "Thank you" and hurry down the other side.

Samuel said there would be a meadow, and as soon as we walk between two trees, we see it. The spring meadow has short clusters of grass and little wildflowers that are white and more that are purple. Taller red and orange flowers dot up here and there, and an eerie calm hangs over the area.

My eyes land on the only irregularity in the meadow.

A ring of mushrooms.

"Are you ready for this?" Garrett asks.

"No," I admit.

"Me neither."

I hold Kai a little tighter. "What if we can't get back?"

Garrett takes my hand. "I'm sure we can negotiate with that ball."

I know he has no more idea than I do how this is going to turn out. But this is our only chance to help Kai. We have to find a fairy.

"Together?" Garrett asks.

My heart is racing and I step up to the edge of the ring. "For Prince Kaison."

"Here we go."

We step into the ring.

# Chapter Thirteen

The sky overhead changes from bright blue to a greenish hue, like the color of robin's egg. All around us, bright flecks of light float in the air. The trees aren't green and brown like they are in our world, but the trunks are more of a rich, deep purple and the leaves have a dull yellow or green glow to them. Everything is more mysterious, but somehow brighter. The very air seems to vibrate with magic in a way I've only felt when touching an enchanted artifact.

I turn to speak with Garrett, only to come face-to-face with Kai.

*Human* Kai.

He is blinking rapidly. Confusion swirls in his gaze and his lips are parted as he sucks in deep breaths.

"Kai!" I throw my arms around his neck, pulling him against me. "Kai! You're you!"

He wraps his arms around me slowly at first. I can't imagine going from the size of a frog to being back to over six feet. Or from losing my mind to frog instincts to suddenly being human.

But everything seems to finally click for him and he drags me against his chest, swallowing me in his embrace.

He buries his face in my neck and inhales. "El. I was so worried. I was losing myself."

"I know. But you're back." I smile.

"I thought if I jumped in the water from the falls I would return to me, but it didn't work."

I rest my feet back on the ground, only to cup his face in my hands so I can look into his copper eyes. Those eyes I fell in love with ages ago. In a time when everything was right. "You actually thought to do that?"

"You thought I just fell in?"

"Well . . . hopped, but yes. You *were* turning more into a frog."

He smiles and places his hands over mine. "I guess getting me here was enough to break the spell."

I recognize his vest is *gold*, his shirt is white, and he wears his ceremonial sword on his waist. He's still in his wedding clothes.

"You didn't change," I blurt.

Kai's tired brows twitch in confusion. "Huh?"

"I mean . . . your clothes. You married her, and you're still in your wedding clothes."

He slowly raises a brow. "Yes?"

"You never . . . slept . . . with her?" I hesitate to ask.

"No." He says it so casually, like he thought I knew it, and then he inclines his head. "El, I married her because I had to."

Garrett clears his throat.

Kai shifts his eyes, and I notice his lips tighten when I drop my hands and turn to see what Garrett wants.

I open my mouth to say something, but Garrett is pointing upward, toward the sky.

It's . . . cracking.

My brows furrow and I turn in a slow circle. Sparkles of gold float down to the ground and the light dims.

"What . . . is happening?" I know neither of them can answer, but I can't keep the question inside.

"Well, well, well. We wouldn't happen to have Prince Kaison, son of King Willard the Seventh, in our midst?"

We all turn and both Kai and Garrett step in front of me. Kai glares at Garrett and elbows him out of the way so *he* is the one protecting me. I can't help but feel a little happy to be fought over, even if it's only a moment.

I lean to look around Kai's shoulder to see a fairy with white hair pulled half up in a bun at the back of his head, dull black-and-gray moth-like wings, and a black uniform with a red emblem on the chest. His eyes are sharp and cold. He is flanked by two other fairies, both with sharp black butterfly wings, in the same uniform but with black hair.

"What do you want?" Kai asks.

The fairy laughs, but his smile doesn't brighten his eyes. He reaches his arms up toward the sky. "Do you not see? You fulfilled our intentions."

Kai's head shifts ever so slightly, and I don't need to see his face to know he's confused.

"What intentions?" Garrett cuts in.

"You don't know?" The fairy's smirk makes me want to slap him. He drags in a deep breath and rests his hands on his hips. "Tsk. Your father never told you the truth?" He meets Kai's gaze and doesn't blink.

Kai rounds his shoulders. "That he made some sort of pact with your sorceress? Yes. He told me that. He wanted children but couldn't have any, so she allowed my mother to have me."

"Oh. Oh, little prince." The fairy chuckles, and it grows into a roar of laughter with the other two fairies joining in with much less enthusiasm.

Garrett places his hand on the hilt of his sword, eyes darting from one to another, ready to move if provoked. It's the first time I've seen him truly in his element as a soldier.

"Oh, you poor thing." The fairy wipes at invisible tears. "Little highness. That's only half of the story."

Cheering echoes through the forest from somewhere in the distance.

Kai reaches back and places his hand on me to make sure I'm there. I reach forward and take his hand, wanting that comfort from him.

"I would ask you to enlighten me," he says, "but it appears we are keeping you from some kind of celebration. Point us in the direction back to my kingdom, and we will leave your land."

"It's not quite so easy." The fairy looks like a court jester the way he's grinning. "You see, you are trespassers in our land. And I happen to know someone who is dying to meet you. Well, officially." He almost giggles and motions his hand for us to follow.

His men part, their hands going to their weapons, and they keep a close eye on Garrett.

"What do you want to do?" Garrett asks softly.

"We don't know the way out," Kai responds under his breath.

"They're arresting us."

"I see that." Kai breaks his concentration on the fairies to look at me. "Stay between Garrett and me."

I nod but don't let go of Kai's hand. Luckily for me, he doesn't try to let go of me either.

"Your weapon." One of them holds out his empty hand.

Garrett reluctantly unbuckles the belt and hands over his sword.

"And your bag."

Garrett's lips tighten as he removes the bag and hands it over. The soldier opens it, rummages around a bit, and then hoists it over his shoulder.

"You?" the other guard asks Kai.

Kai is still in his wedding clothing, which means he has only his ceremonial sword, and he hands it over as well. His eyes are narrowed and he looks like he might strike the guard in spite of having no weapon, but he refrains.

"Little miss?" the first guard asks me.

I raise my brow. "Do I look like I have a weapon?"

"We need to search your pouch." His tone lets me know it's not up for debate, and it's clear to me that we are not in a position to argue.

I blink and look down at Acorn's pouch. "This? I have a hedgehog. Can I take him out?"

The fairy glances at the leader, brow twitching. "General Nizra?"

Nizra chuckles. "You chose a hedgehog as your familiar? Let me check." He holds out his hand for my pouch.

I hold my breath. If he gets the ball, we have no leverage. "He's going to be frightened." When the fairy doesn't move, I reluctantly hand it over.

The fairy chuckles. "There is, indeed, a hedgehog in here. Hello."

"Who are you? Where is Elowyn?" Acorn's voice shouts up at him.

"She's right here and quite well." He closes the bag and hands it back to me. "It's wise to have healing potions, especially where you're going. Follow us. And don't worry, we only bite on Thursdays. Is today Thursday?" He glances back. "Oops." He traces my figure with his eyes, deliberately looking me down and then back up before he winks.

I raise my finger in a crude gesture.

He snorts. "She's got fire. No wonder the two off you are fighting over her."

Kai's hand tightens on mine.

"Are we okay?" Acorn asks.

I glance down to see him poking his head from the side of the bag. "I don't know," I admit.

"I can hear him," Garrett comments softly. "I mean I understand Acorn." He smiles. "Hello, Acorn." He looks at the hedgehog and offers a little wave. I can't help but think he's trying to help keep me calm, and I hate even more that the simple act is actually working.

Acorn's nose twitches with excitement. "I can talk to you now, Whiskers?"

He nods.

"Oh good! Next time you choose caterpillars, leave the yellow ones. They are bitter. Like onions."

Garrett chuckles. "I'll keep that in mind."

We walk with the fairies through the forest, the trees looking very much like the forest we were just in, which ends at the crest of a hill. They don't pause to admire their city, but I do. I thought fairies were small and lived in lanterns or abandoned animal holes. That's what the images in books depict. A beautiful city of structures made of polished and carved wood with several stories to them was not what I imagined. The architecture rivals that of the city of Parshen where we live. Different types of trees have been used to give depth to the buildings in dark and light colors.

People fill the streets, dancing and celebrating. They wear clothes like ours, but of finer quality. The women's dresses flow with ethereal lightness, and the men's tunics and trousers hug them to show every muscle of their toned bodies. But everything is carefully designed around their stunning wings. Unlike the soldiers currently escorting us, most of the fairies have brightly colored wings, making the streets a kaleidoscope of color flickering on the trees and buildings surrounding them.

I suddenly feel very naked and wish I had stayed in my sopping wet dress over being in my very obviously worn under dress. I wrap my arm around myself and step closer to Kai.

"Are you all right?" he whispers.

"Keep going." One of the black-haired soldiers pushes me.

Kai immediately releases my hand to wrap his arm around my shoulders and glares at the man. "Don't touch her. She's capable of walking on her own. You don't need to show her such rudeness."

The man doesn't seem intimidated at all by Kai's posturing.

"We can't take on all of the fairies at once, Your Highness," Garrett warns.

Kai relaxes only enough to allow me to continue walking. But he's still tense. I feel it in his arm and side, which I haven't moved from.

When I glance at Garrett, he is watching me from the corner of his eye. When our gazes meet, he quickly looks away. He looks almost hurt.

The celebration of the fairies changes when we enter the city. The cheers dull to shock, and a whisper like the wind begins to build into a murmur and then thunder. The fairies push in toward us as the word spreads that humans are in the land.

Garrett presses against my other side. I notice he has broadened his shoulders and has no issues holding his arm out to push curious fairies back as they lean in to get a look at Kai.

"It's true!"

"He's here!"

"He's broken the binding!"

"The second-born has been brought."

"The vow is fulfilled."

"What do they mean?" I ask, afraid to look away from the fairies.

"Second-born?" Kai mutters.

Nizra chuckles, the tone dark. "All will be explained when you get to the prison. This way." He raises his hands. "Please create a path. I'm certain our lovely Genoa will put him on display shortly. Thank you."

The crowd parts just enough to allow us through, but both Kai and Garrett have to push them further back. More than once, Kai has to yank his arm free from a fairy.

My heart is pounding so loudly I am certain everyone nearby can hear. We're going to a prison. For so long, I've tried to avoid this very thing and now I walk on shaking legs toward one in a fairy realm. Is it safer than the one Mother is locked in? Did Mother feel this same panic when she was led to her cell?

A million questions burn in my mind, and I know the men on either side of me must have at least as many questions as I do. It's too loud and chaotic for any of them to be answered, though.

"Breathe," Kai says softly. "In through your nose, out through your mouth."

I glance up at him. How does he know what I feel?

"You're pale," he explains. "And you're shaking like a leaf. In through your nose, out through your mouth."

I suck in a short breath through my nose and blast it out from my mouth. I repeat it, the next time managing to breathe in slower, and the third one is far more controlled. I've never felt more grateful to be beside someone who knows me so well.

We are led to a tree wider than any tree I've seen in my life. In fact, it's nearly the width of my home. A black door has been carved into it, and Nizra places his palm on a carved square before whispering something I can't hear.

The lock clicks and he pulls the door open. He winks once again at me and gestures for us to enter.

None of us move.

It's my turn to tighten my grip on Kai's hand, because I feel a wave of magic and darkness wash over me the instant the door opens. It hits me like a frigid wind and my breath catches.

"El?" Kai whispers.

"Do you want to make a scene?" the fairy asks.

"I'll take up the rear," Garrett states. His hand brushes mine and I blink and glance at him. "Breathe," he whispers.

I gulp a breath and then swallow. "Thank you."

He nods.

Kai steps forward, pulling me behind him, again without letting go of my hand. I feel like I'm not only being dragged physically with Kai, but emotionally. I felt my heart jump when Garret touched my hand, but having Kai take control feels comforting as well.

"Pity. I wanted a show." The leader steps in first, followed by Kai, me, and then Garrett.

I am momentarily blinded, stepping from bright sunlight to darkness lit only by a handful of floating, glowing orbs. Nearly ten fairy soldiers stand in the room. It must be a space for them to guard the entrance of the prison, as there are chairs and a small kitchen. A ladder built into one wall leads up to what might be a sleeping loft.

"Everyone, meet little Prince Kaison."

The guards' eyes widen. "He's here?"

"We heard people cheering. Does this mean the binding is broken?"

They all exchange hopeful looks.

"Indeed." The fairy plucks one of the floating orbs from the air. The light inside brightens at his touch, further illuminating the space surrounding us. "This way, our lovely guests." He descends a staircase I hadn't seen beyond Kai.

The staircase is tight and spirals downward for what feels like miles. It's likely only a short distance, but I'm terrified and it's dark. The lower we go, the colder it becomes, and I'm currently in a dress with no sleeves. I don't want to say anything as I begin to shiver.

"Hold a moment," Garrett says.

"And why?" the fairy snaps.

Garrett doesn't respond. He instead removes his cloak and drapes it around me. The warmth instantly subdues my goosebumps, and I pull it closer. He nods silently.

I smile back.

Kai's eyes darken. I know it must be from jealousy, but he has no cloak to offer me.

"Oh, you three really need a bedroom." Nizra dramatically rolls his eyes and continues our descent.

My cheeks flush and I look down.

Once we reach flat ground, there is another door to walk through. Again, the fairy places his palm on it and whispers before it opens. This reveals a long bridge over a chasm so deep I can't see the bottom and so high I can't see the top. My breath hitches. Bridges crisscross at every level, and there are bars on this side to show the prisoners inside.

"See that cell right there?" He points to a vacant cell directly across from where we stand. We can look right into it from here. He looks at Kai. "That was designated to you nineteen years ago."

"What do you mean?" Kai asks, his voice deep.

"When your father broke his vow and bound us to our realm, Genoa's plans changed. Of course, if he had just fulfilled his promise and given you to Genoa when he was supposed to, you would have been raised as royalty here. Now, you get to be on display for her collection instead." He pats Kai on the shoulder. "Don't worry. She'll soon be here to explain everything in better detail."

My mind reels. Kai was *supposed* to be raised here? With the fairies? What did Nizra mean?

Kai doesn't move and his face remains stoic, but his grip on my hand flexes and I can sense his sudden nervousness.

I try to comfort him by squeezing his hand, but he doesn't look down at me.

We cross the bridge and turn to the right into a hallway, and Nizra opens the door to what he told us is Kai's cell. Kai hesitates and then pulls me with him.

"Ah, ah. She has a cell all of her own." The fairy snatches my free arm.

"She comes with me," Kai insists, eyes narrowing. He stands to his full height and steps toward the fairy. "She stays with me."

"I'm afraid that isn't allowed. You can't fight me here, boy." The fairy's eyes narrow and his demeanor shifts as his eyes darken. "You don't want her hurt, do you?"

"Put me in a cell with Garrett and I'll go willingly," I say.

"If I can't be with Kai, I can be with him." I look at Kai, hoping he can see that I'll still be safe with Garrett.

Kai's jaw flexes. "As long as she stays with him, I'll let her go."

The fairy chuckles. "Fine. She stays with the soldier."

Kai pulls me close. "I'm so sorry I got you into this mess," he whispers. "I'm sorry I hurt you. I'm sorry I failed to keep you safe and broke your trust and . . . your heart."

I wrap my arms around him, overwhelmed by a rush of emotions. My chest feels like it might explode from hope and sadness. I'm afraid of what is going to happen.

He places his lips on my forehead, then hooks his finger under my chin.

My breath catches—but then I'm rudely pulled away. The fairy shoves Kai back and into his cell. His room is on an outer wall that is nothing but iron bars with sharp designs securing them together and to the ceiling and floor. Beyond that wall is the open space from which we entered. Sunlight fills his cell, and I can make out the shape of a bed. The door slides closed from somewhere in the wall, a door of bars with a short gap at the bottom.

The cell across from Kai's unlocks and rolls open. Nizra doesn't let go of my arm. Instead, his fingers squeeze tightly.

Garrett doesn't budge. "Ladies first." He's not looking at me, though. I am very aware he isn't going to move until he knows I'll actually be in the cell with him.

The fairy must pick up on it, because he sneers. "You are

so polite."

"She goes first," Garrett insists.

Nizra snorts and pulls my arm up, forcing me to step close to him. He sniffs my hair. "You're a weak magic user. Possibly with potential, but goodness, you've been suppressed. It must be miserable for you to be in Parshen. Here, we can give you real power. Real strength."

"Let me go," I say firmly, but inside I tremble.

He chuckles. "You're so ignorant. It's a pity you're wasted on them." He shoves me backward and into the cell, causing me to stumble and fall.

Garrett steps in behind me and faces Nizra, using his body as a shield until the door is closed and locked.

"We'll see you soon!" The fairy waves, turns, and disappears around the corner.

Our cell is much darker, as we have no windows or lanterns and the only light comes from our door. We also have no bed.

Garrett turns to me and helps me to my feet. "Are you hurt?"

"No." I tremble and lean my back against the wall, finally breathing normally for the first time since entering the fairy realm.

"Your ribs are fine?"

I hadn't even noticed the pain was gone until he mentioned it. "The water from the falls must have healed them. I'm fine," I insist when he doesn't change his expression. "What in the four winds is going on?"

Garrett turns to look through the bars at Kai. "Is there something you haven't told us?"

Kai shakes his head, jaw still tight, and he walks to the back of his cell, which overlooks the chasm. "Clearly there's something even I wasn't told. I have a feeling this is much worse than any of us realize."

## Chapter Fourteen

I sit with my back against the wall and my knees pulled to my chest, desperate for what little heat I can gain. My gown is still damp, allowing the cold of the prison to penetrate in spite of Garrett's cloak. My teeth begin to chatter.

Garrett has been investigating the locks and hinges, prying at each opening, but the door is impenetrable. He lets out a sigh and mutters, "It's probably enchanted anyway" under his breath. He turns and looks me up and down. "You're shivering again." He doesn't hesitate to sit at my side. "Mind if I help?" He wraps his arms around me, immediately enveloping me in his warmth.

"I f-feel so c-cold." I lean into him. It's strange how we irritated one another just a little while ago and now I'm snuggled up against him, my emotions torn between him and Kai.

I'm not sure whether or not it is intentional, but he rubs his hand up and down my arm in a slow motion, clearly trying to keep me warm. "I'm sorry he's hurt you."

I immediately tense and look sideways at him.

"I just mean that, to me, you deserve someone who wouldn't pledge a life of loyalty to another woman and then claim he still cares for you." Concern pinches his brows.

"Kai is . . . so much more than just someone I care about." I shift so I can look at Garrett a little better. "I grew up known as the daughter of the witch of the woods. It didn't always have a bad connotation at first, but having a purple eye made me stand out from everyone else. I didn't have non-magic friends until I was past five, and the first person to play with me was Samuel's daughter."

Garrett's gaze searches my face as he listens.

I continue. "One day, I was maybe six? I was in the city with Mother, and she stepped into a shop to pick something up. I had a pocket of beautiful stones I had collected and was laying them out so I could see how the sun shined on them. A group of children spotted me and asked to play." I smile bitterly at the memory. "Mother hadn't been gone terribly long. She was only stepping in to pick up the lovely purple hat I had left behind. I was so excited that other children wanted to play with me. But the instant I stood up, one of them asked me what happened to my eye. Their friend said I was the *little witch that lives in the pond*. They started calling me a bog witch and teased me that I smelled like one. They stole my rocks and blocked me from getting to my mother."

"That's awful."

"It was." I smile softly. "Until this bigger kid showed up and shoved the meanest one to the ground. He demanded my rocks back and told them to go away." I find my attention drift to Kai's cell.

His dark eyes meet mine and his lips curl into a soft smile, acknowledging that he's heard me and remembers too.

"Kai?" Garrett replies.

I nod.

Garrett leans his head back. "He was your protector."

"He always has been. He followed me home. I don't know why, but after he knew where I lived, he always showed up to play. He tried to get his friends to play with me too, but it wasn't the same sort of feeling. They played with me because they *had* to. Because the prince had asked. As the years passed, they distanced themselves but Kai remained consistent. How is any of that bad?"

"Friendship isn't bad," Garrett clarified. "I just fear you won't be happy because of what he's done to you. Does he know everything about you? Down to your favorite flower?"

I smile a little and lean forward across Garrett to call out. "Kai?"

"Yes?" he answers back.

"What is my favorite flower?"

He hesitates in confusion and then says, "Uh, well, I would say that's a trick question. In the spring, you love your hyacinths, but they don't last all season, so you always have those ball flowers." He makes the shape with his hand.

Heat crawls up my cheek. I didn't even know he realized this much about me. "They're called hydrangeas." I find myself twisting hair around my finger.

Kai's handsome smile slides onto his lips. "Hydrangea. I'll have to remember that better."

I look over at Garrett, who isn't looking at either of us. "I understand that you mean well," I say softly. "But I can't stop Kai from being my closest friend."

"Did he *have* to marry Princess Genoa?" Garrett finally lifts his gaze to me.

I bite my lip.

"You know I can hear you, right?" Kai says from across the hall.

Garrett sighs. "It was easier to have conversations when he was just a frog."

I look across Garrett to Kai leaning his shoulder against the bars of his cell. "I can't change the laws unless I am the king, and the only way to become king is through marriage," Kai explains.

"But nowhere in our laws does it say you are required to marry a princess."

Kai's jaw flexes. "My father arranged a political marriage to a princess who we thought belonged to a neighboring kingdom, and I agreed because I couldn't have the girl I wanted anyway." He looks at me and then slowly tears his gaze away. "A part of me knew she would never actually forgive me, and I still had to marry."

"You wouldn't even fight for her?"

"You have no idea what I've done for her," Kai replies

coldly, his eyes narrowed. "You may be a soldier and a spy for my father, but you have no way of knowing everything that happens in the castle."

"I don't need to in order to see what you've done to Elowyn."

"You barely met her!"

"Peacocks! You're both beautiful!" Nizra is back. "Or shall I obtain a looking glass so you can compare the size of your muscles and choose a winner once and for all?"

Garrett and Kai have matching scowls.

I use the opportunity of the distraction to pull away from Garrett, leaving his cloak behind, and cross to the cell door with my arms wrapped around myself. "I don't suppose you would be willing to get me something more appropriate to wear? My dress got wet and I left it behind."

The fairy smirks. He struts over and leans against the cell door inches from me. "Hm. I suppose I could do that, but you'd have to do something for me in return."

I roll my eyes. "Seriously? I have to listen to these two argue and now you're joining in to barter?"

He shakes his head. "It's not like that. See, we fairies like to collect things that intrigue us. For Genoa, impressive creatures or people are her thing. Me?" He raises his hand, which is decorated with rings. He turns his palm toward himself so I can see the jewels.

No.

Eyes.

My breath snags.

One is yellow and slitted, like a reptile's. Another is humanoid and a lovely shade of green. The third is blue.

"Your stunning purple eye would be the perfect addition to my collection. Don't you think?" He wiggles his fingers.

I slowly raise my eyebrow. "You want to pluck out my eye and put it on a ring?"

"Yes." He grins. "And then I'll bring you all of the clothes you can ask for."

"You're disgusting." I turn away and sit in the far corner with my knees pulled to my chest once again.

"Pity." The fairy clicks his tongue. "I can also throw in magic training. Genoa is the most powerful sorceress our people have ever seen. Imagine learning from the best. You might become half the sorceress she is."

I scoff. "Why would I want to train under someone who has imprisoned us?"

"Only momentarily." He grins wider.

"I'm fine being ignorant," I snark back. Why would I train under Kai's new wife? What torture would that be?

He chuckles. "I like you." He straightens and holds up manacles. "We are here to escort you all to your meeting."

The doors slide open, and two fairy guards step into Kai's cell at the same time two step into ours. One comes toward me, but Garrett blocks him. The fairy doesn't hesitate to deliver a blow to the side of his head. Being a king's guard, he could have blocked it, and I wonder why he doesn't.

"Know your place," the guard orders. He steps past Garrett and commands me to put out my wrists.

I notice Garrett watching over his shoulder as his own wrists are chained together behind his back. I hold out my wrists and the icy metal is clamped around them.

We are led beyond the entrance and up a flight of stairs with a barred door at the top. Nizra uses his touch to unlock it, like he did on the way into the prison, and we are taken through the small office into the hallway. We must be in some kind of barracks because the wall to our left is lined with windows. The sunlight and sounds of celebration in the distance fill the space, but I don't even get an opportunity to try to see what is beyond the window because we are immediately forced into another room.

The room might have been a library if it weren't for the broad table covered in a map with carved figurines upon it. An enormous window spills light down on the map.

Genoa smiles brightly from where she stands. "Darling! I've missed you!" She walks around the side of the table, directly to Kai.

He bristles and the muscle of his jaw tightens.

She cups his face and kisses him. "You've been gone too long. I was worried you got lost in a pond somewhere." She raises a brow. "No greeting for your wife?"

"What do you want?" he asks, his voice deep.

She grins. "Nizra tells me you don't know the truth of

the vow your parents made to me. Or how they broke that promise and bound all fairies to this realm."

Kai's expression remains cold.

My nose begins to tickle and I wiggle it. Now is the wrong time to sneeze and draw attention.

Genoa, in a flowing pink gown, takes Kai's hand and pulls him to a chair. "Let me show you."

Kai walks with her but refuses the seat. "I can stand."

"I insist." Her eyes narrow and her grin somehow becomes . . . sharp.

He slowly sits.

"Good." She pats his cheek and turns to the table. "Your parents were desperate for a child. What can a king do with no one to carry on his line? They considered a surrogate, but your laws would then allow the other woman's family rights to wealth and social standing your parents didn't want to part with. Sorcerers, sorceresses, wizards, and witches came through offering their non-solutions." She moves her hands and a life-like, translucent blue image of the castle appears hovering over the map. People walk in and out of the main entrance.

"I know all of this," Kai states.

Her brow twitches. "Did you know about this?"

An image of Kai's father—far younger and without his beard—takes form standing beside the queen.

"We have no other options," his father says. "We have attempted every solution and nothing works."

Genoa stands across from them, looking very much the same as she does now. "I can help you, but you must give me something in return."

"Anything. We'll do anything," Kai's mother pleads.

"I will grant you the blessing to bear as many children as you wish to. But you will give me your firstborn in return."

The king and queen exchange worried glances.

Kai's stoic expression shifts into confusion. I can almost read his mind. If they were supposed to give their firstborn, why is he here? And does that mean he has a sibling?

The king shakes his head. "We cannot offer the first. By law, they must take the throne."

"Then you shall give me your second."

Kai's lips tighten.

"Only, he didn't give you to me," Genoa explains. She steps between Kai's knees and leans back against the table.

He shakes his head. "I had a sibling?"

"A brother." She heaves a dramatic sigh. "He died some months after his birth. Your parents never told you?" She reaches out and strokes his cheek.

He slaps her hand away. "Don't touch me."

She laughs. "You're bound to me now, foolish human." She holds her hand—and wedding ring—inches from his face. "I came the day after you were born to collect you, and they refused to hand you over. Your mother told me you had to be the one to take the throne, so they would give me the next. But vows don't work that way." She nudges herself closer and presses one hand to the back of Kai's seat so he has no choice but to lean back in his chair. "Vows don't work that way," she repeats slowly, deliberately. "You may not appreciate it now, but you'll realize how good this is for you."

"That doesn't explain how we ended up here," Garrett states.

Genoa slowly lifts her gaze and her blue eyes are practically black. I swear her teeth are becoming pointed as we watch. "They never gave me Kai. Instead, they used every magic user they could and sacrificed them to bind us here."

"My father wouldn't do something like that." Kai pushes against Genoa and goes to stand, but she grabs him by the throat and shoves him back in place.

"Your father bartered with your life before you were even born. What makes you think he wouldn't murder innocent magic wielders to better serve his purpose?"

"How do I know any part of this is true?" he counters. "That you haven't fabricated this to make me hate my father?"

Her lip twitches. "You already hate your father. Telling you any of this simply explains further why he is the way he is. The only way to break the binding was to fulfil my vow. To get you here, in our realm. I'm sure you all noticed the celebrations in the land? I used the magical orb to gain access into your realm and turn you into a frog so I could easily transport you home. A farce marriage was the only way I could get you alone."

Kai scoffs and tries to pull her hand off, but she stands strong.

"I turned you into a frog so I could bring you here. I knew I would never be able to convince you to willingly step into a fairy ring, and no one would notice you as a frog. When you escaped and the little witch showed up"—her eyes lock on me—"it was inconvenient that you changed the path in which you arrived, but it has still worked in my favor. You had no idea you were helping banish your love."

"There must be an arrangement we can make now," Kai says, his voice calm, but I see how tense he is sitting.

Genoa's lips curl in a cruel grin. She finally releases Kai's throat and strokes his cheek with her knuckles. "You want to go home so soon? I imagine you miss the comfort of your bed. How does it feel being human again?"

"Not for me. For them. Let them go. You have what you want with me."

Genoa taps her chin and looks Garrett up and down, and then me. "I'm thinking that guard might make a rather good labor slave. We have so few of such caliber. Would you like him in my kingdom?" She laughs in an icy tone.

"Can I keep the girl?" Nizra asks. He licks his lips. "She smells delicious."

I step up to Garrett's back. With his wrists chained behind him, all he can do is reach out and grasp my fingers, which tremble as I cling to the only source of comfort I have in this place.

Genoa tilts her head. "I don't see why not. I have no use of her. She's pathetically weak." Genoa returns her attention to Kai. "But not quite yet. There is one thing I must do before I return to fetch you. Give me a day, Nizra." She grips Kai's chin and kisses him yet again. "I'll see you soon, my love." Genoa steps back and snaps her fingers.

The fairy guards rush forward and lift Kai from the seat by his arms, then roughly drag him from the room. Garrett and I are shoved from behind, directed to follow until we are delivered back to our cells.

Nizra watches while the others unlock our chains. He then claps his hands before rubbing them together. "Since you're here for at least a day, we shall review the rules of Ipten Prison. You will be granted four hours each day in the courtyard, two in the morning and two in the evening. We find *some* sunlight keeps the violence down. You will return to your cells when you are instructed. Your only warning is to follow the rules and you *should* survive the night. One of those breaks is about to happen. Good luck!" He winks at me and the doors glide closed, locking us back inside.

Kai slowly turns away and leans against the bars on the far side of his cell. I can't imagine the confusion he feels having just learned he had a brother he didn't know about, his parents had gifted him to the fairies, and his father only wanted to keep him to maintain the throne.

Kai looks absolutely broken.

And I have no way to comfort him.

## Chapter Fifteen

There is a click above our cells that echoes in a rhythmic pattern down the hall before the doors simultaneously slide open. The slotted doors disappear into the stone walls.

"Stay close to us," Garrett says to me. He holds out his cloak to me.

I glance at Kai, who hasn't moved, and accept the cloak. "Are you coming with us?"

Garrett steps out first, surveying left and right, and then steps further to the left, blocking the hall, and motions for me to exit.

Kai steps out of the cell without looking at either one of us, and he lingers long enough for me to slip into the hall behind him. I hold Garrett's cloak around my body for warmth and some degree of modesty. Not knowing what else to do, I reach my hand out and brush it against Kai's, which hangs at his hip.

He doesn't reciprocate and my heart breaks a little more.

A blue man with a single eye on his head pushes past us, shoving Kai into the wall as he does so. He grumbles, "Watch it."

"Cyclops," Garrett whispers behind me. "They're a barbaric race known for eating humans."

"You've seen them before?" I ask.

"Yes. When I worked border control. They live in the Volcano Ring. More than once they've entered our borders and destroyed villages."

Other beings fill the hall—beings with hunched backs and creatures no taller than my knee who must have been goblins, but a majority of them are fairies. Their wings are wrinkled and limp, and their faces are nothing short of nightmares. Their eyes are narrow and black, their noses long and pointed like their chins.

The entire space is filled with the noise of shuffling feet, grumbling voices, and somewhere far behind us, someone screams. I bite my lip and step closer to Kai.

Kai turns his head to speak over his shoulder. "I've heard of fairies losing their purity, but I didn't know what happened to them."

"What do you mean, losing purity?" Garret asks.

"Committing enough evil acts that eventually their soul withers away, as does the essence of who they once were." He nudges his head toward a fairy tapping his nails together as he studies us.

"And apparently they end up here," Garrett replies. He presses up against my back right as a figure with flowing robes and blue manacles floats by. "This must be a prison for the very dangerous."

"Then why would they put *us* here?" I mutter.

Garrett shrugs. "Maybe they're hoping we can die here and they can blame it on a monster instead of taking responsibility?"

I look at Garrett.

He shrugs.

"That's an awful thing to say."

"He's right," Kai replies shortly. "Stay close."

The hall turns here and there until it ends at a tall doorway with a pointed portcullis hanging overhead, threatening to drop any moment. We step out into the blinding sunlight, and I place my hand on Kai's back to follow him. The sunlight sends a wave of ache through my head. It's late in the day, but the sun shines right down on us.

When my eyes have adjusted, I see hundreds of monsters and beings in the heavily guarded space. The walls tower above us and are made of black stone I know must be incredibly thick. But at the very top of the hole we are in, there are trees. This prison is very much underground. If I had a prison, it would probably be in a hole. If anyone riots, all they have to do is break one of the walls and the earth will bury everyone.

I shudder at the thought.

A creature with a man's torso and the tail of a snake instead of legs approaches us. "New meat." He flicks a forked tongue.

"Back off, naga," Kai says firmly. "We don't want any trouble."

It laughs. "You've sseen my kind, have you?"

"I'm really not in the mood. And I don't need a sword to protect myself."

The naga raises his hands in the air innocently. "Relax. I only wanted to ssay hello. But you may wish to keep both eyess open. You must taste deliciouss." He smirks and turns to slither back into the crowd.

"Think we're going to survive until your wife comes back?" Garrett mutters under his breath.

Kai snaps a glare at him. "Of course we will."

I swallow hard, which is difficult considering how dry my throat is. "I think I would rather stay in the cell."

If I were an elf or bogart, I might not draw any attention at all, but being newcomers, human, *and* having Kai with us makes me feel like we are standing naked in the center of a city. Everyone is watching us with calculated glances.

Others walk by, staring us down, getting our scent, and eventually backing us against the wall. Garrett and Kai remain forward, both looking intimidating in my eyes. Luckily, their stances seem enough to keep most back.

A buzz reverberates through the prison, a low tone I don't know if Kai or Garrett can hear, because I recognize the feeling of magic. Dark magic. It tastes like lightning threatening to strike at any moment.

Until a fairy approaches us. He wears a black pair of

trousers, shirt, and vest. He is the first fairy I have seen in the prison who actually still looks like a fairy. His wings are orange that fades to a beautiful red, and the design is outlined with black. His hair is also a bright orange. It must have some sort of significance, because the fallen fairies all have black hair and colorless wings. Most importantly, a piece of leather covers his left eye.

"You must be the cause of all of the commotion in the land." He extends his hand. "I am Temarilian, but you may call me Tem. It's easier."

Kai doesn't move. "What do you want?"

"To be frank? I'm the only way you're going to get out." He tilts his chin up confidently.

Kai folds his arms across his chest. "Forgive me for not trusting you immediately. It's been a bad day."

The fairy finally drops his hand. "Ah. Forgive me. I noticed your friend is terribly underdressed." His gaze darts to me. "I am only offering clothing she can have."

It sounds wonderful to me, but neither of my protectors moves.

"Why help us?" Kai asks.

"Because, believe it or not, I've been waiting for you for years," the fairy replies. His voice remains cautious and low. "Genoa is a brilliant sorceress, but she has allowed jealousy and hatred to blind her. She let her hatred grow and consume her. I know you want to get out of here, and so do I. I need to help her and therefore escape is mutually beneficial."

"You know her?" Garrett asks.

He nods.

"And why would *you* think you can help her?" Kai counters.

"I want to reach her before it's too late. You see, fairies are creatures of light." He gestures to his wings. "Color. Joy. Curiosity. When hatred seizes our hearts, that purity and light disappears."

Realization dawns on me. "Her colors are dull."

His eyes dart to me. "You've seen her?"

All three of us nod.

"How was she?" His brows soften into concern.

"Her wings are orange," I say. "But they've faded. I didn't realize it until seeing you."

His shoulders drop.

"But she's still blonde and beautiful." I don't know how that can help, but at least she doesn't look like the monsters looming behind Tem. I clear my throat. "How do fairies become evil enough to turn into that?"

He glances over his shoulder and then faces us again. "*That* is what happens when fairies accept their darkness."

"And will she fall that far?" Garrett asks.

Tem draws in a slow breath. "I would like to prevent that from happening. Based on what you're describing, she doesn't have too much longer. We should go to my cell. Your friend can change, and we can get away from eavesdroppers."

Kai shakes his head stubbornly. "I'm sorry, but I have no reason to trust you just because you say we should."

I can't blame him for not trusting anything at this moment. I can't help but reach up and rub the side of my head as my temple pulses against the bright sun.

"Are you all right?" Garrett asks, placing his hand on my back.

I nod. "Just a little headache."

He exhales. "Other than falling into the river, you haven't had a proper drink of water in a while. Is there somewhere to get water?" he asks Tem.

The fairy nods and moves through the crowd.

"Did you notice how everyone moves for him?" Kai murmurs.

"I did," Garrett replies. "And notice how the soldier straightened and bowed when he approached?"

"Are you implying he's important?" I ask.

Kai sighs, his shoulders finally loosening. "I don't know." He reaches his hand up and runs his fingers through his hair. "I'm probably reading into it. This place . . ." He finally turns his back to the creatures in the large space to look at me properly. His gaze flickers over me. He then turns to Garrett. "Promise me something."

"Yes sir?"

Kai grabs the front of Garrett's shirt and leans so he's inches from Garrett's face. "If you get the chance to escape, you take Elowyn with you. Understand? Take her and keep her safe."

I stare at him in disbelief. "What makes you think we're leaving you behind?"

"It's an order," Kai says firmly, eyes still locked with Garrett's.

"I understand." He nods once. "I'll do as you say."

Kai releases him.

"Excuse me?" I scowl up at them. "We aren't leaving you behind. If we even get a chance to do any of that."

Kai turns away from me.

"What, now you're going to ignore me? You give him an order and pretend I'm no longer here?"

"He's trying to keep you safe," Garrett tries. He reaches for me, but I slap his hand away.

"See, that's what he does best. He turns his back on me and then says it's to keep me safe." I shove Garrett's cloak against his chest, giving it back, and grab Kai's arm and turn him. "You and I have been avoiding one another for long enough. If you have something to say, say it."

Kai surveys the area. "You want to do this right here? Right now?"

"When else are we going to? When you get back to your wife? After Garrett is sold? When I'm given to that fairy for who knows what?" I tighten my hands into fists.

Kai drops his arms to his sides, and Garrett steps away but remains close in case something should happen.

"I know I should have spoken to you months ago," I say to Kai, my voice low. "I should have asked you about your intentions and demanded an explanation and given you a chance to talk when you came over and over." I suck in a breath because the dam holding back my flood of emotions is cracking and I'm not about to let them gush out. I wipe at my face. "I should have stopped you the day of your wedding. I should have forgiven you and told you to leave and come with me." I turn away because the dam is breaking. I can't be weak here! Not in this place! "I keep . . . ruining things. I pushed away the only friend I have, I pushed away Samuel and his family, I haven't even . . ."

Kai catches my arm when I go to turn away. "You haven't ruined anything. Well, except for that one hunting trip where you let the rabbit go."

I look up at him and recall when I was picking blueberries in the woods and heard an animal crying for help. I ran and found it caught in a snare at the same time Kai reached it with his personal bodyguard. Kai told me that was his catch, and I scolded him for trying to hurt an innocent rabbit. He argued it was for his dinner, which mortified me. Of course I released the rabbit. Then we spent several minutes yelling at one another until he finally agreed to come to the cottage and eat something better than a rabbit.

That was the first time my mother actually met him.

I finally find the ability to swallow. "I don't like to talk about how I feel because it doesn't ever help. Who cares that I've been terrified all year? That I'm afraid to be alone? I'm afraid of what will happen if the snow gets too high or if the roof breaks, or if there's a leak in the window I can't fix. And no one is going to want to be my husband because I'm a freak with a purple eye and magic in a country that hates it. What good does it do me for anyone to know that?" I pull away from him.

"Wait. Please." His voice is tight, but he lets me step away for space. "I'm more to blame than you." His tone is full of sadness. "I avoided telling you how I felt all these years. I let my father dictate my life instead of standing up to him. Everything he did in retaliation against you was because of me."

I face him and rub my arm. "Were you ever happy?" I ask.

"What do you mean?"

"As a child. Were you happy?"

"Every moment with you, I was." He smiles his old, familiar smile.

"I should have told you ages ago how I feel," I mutter.

"Well, you *did* offer me a chance to escape with you the morning of my wedding. I was the fool who went through with it. Elowyn." His voice cracks. He lifts my chin to see his eyes brimming with tears. "I am so sorry."

I wish I could change the past. Maybe there is a rune

that can take us back? Time magic is dangerous, though. Even I know that, as illiterate as I am.

A man covered in black fur, just taller than Kai and with much wider shoulders, passes by. But in doing so, he slams his shoulder into Kai's, shoving him hard into the stone wall. He throws a glare over his shoulder. "Pathetic human. Always in the way."

My eyes widen.

His face is that of a wolf.

Kai growls in return and steps toward the wolf man. "What do you want? You had to have come over here and deliberately run into me?"

The wolf sizes up Kai. He grins a dangerous smile. "I wondered how long it would take you to want to fight." He rolls his shoulders forward, making his muscles bulge, and flashes his fangs.

"I'll defend myself." Kai's initial anger calms, but his tone is still dangerous. "And those I care for."

The wolf's eyes flash to me. "Ah. They aren't worth your own life. Trusting women is what got me here. But that doesn't mean I don't want to see what you can do."

Garrett steps up to Kai's side. "He isn't exactly alone."

"Ooh. Two humans. I'm nervous now." He tilts his head back and lets out a laugh that ends in a howl. "Let's see what you've got." He opens his hands by his sides and his claws curl.

"Kai. Garrett. Stop. This is dangerous," I plead. I grab

their arms. "We don't need a fight right now," I say, looking at the wolf. "We're all exhausted and only want a little bit of sunlight."

"I think your men want to show you who might be the better mate." His grin widens across his wolf face and he lets out a growl. "When it proves to be me, you will move to my cell."

Kai's pent-up anger and frustration boil over. He rushes the wolf and slams his shoulder into the creature's sternum.

The wolf takes a shocked step back and gasps a breath, but quickly reacts by driving his elbow down on Kai's back, followed by wrapping an arm around his neck.

"Kai!" I yell.

Garrett dodges the wolf's clawed hand as it slashes out at him and slips under to wrap his own arm around the wolf's neck and shoulder, pinning his arm up against the side of his head and forcing the wolf to bend to the side.

The wolf's growl rumbles deep and he reaches back, grabs Garrett, and throws him over his shoulder and into the crowd.

"Watch it!" someone shouts.

"Mind your business!" another snarls as it kicks Garrett in the head.

The wolf grabs Kai's arm and throws him over his shoulder, slamming his back against the ground. I hear the air explode from Kai's lungs.

I am about to reach into my pouch in search of

something I can at least throw to aid in the fight when a cold hand clamps over my mouth and another grips my wrist and twists until my arm is up behind my back.

"You're coming with me, little one," a voice whispers in my ear as I'm dragged backward.

## Chapter Sixteen

I kick my feet, desperately trying to make noise and draw the attention of Kai or Garrett, but Kai is shielding his face from the wolf's blows and Garrett has only just gotten to his feet and is distracted blocking attacks at his ribs. I try kicking backward, but it's futile as I'm being dragged.

As soon as the shadows of the building cover us, the being spins me around and slams me up against the wall. It's one of the sharp-toothed fairies. His hand remains firm over my mouth and he grins as he presses his hips against mine.

I raise my free hand to slap him, but he snatches my wrist with a chuckle, uncovering my mouth.

"You are alone and unprotected, little one. What brings you to our lovely home?" His voice sounds like boots on gravel. He leans into my neck and sniffs his nose up my jaw, making me cringe and struggle. "You smell absolutely delectable. No wonder those two were trying to keep a close eye on you."

"Get off of me," I say through gritted teeth. I try to raise my knee but can't get enough leverage to deliver any amount of pain, and it only makes the fairy laugh—if you could call it that. With my free hand, I grab his jaw and push it away from me, digging my nails in and tearing them at his flesh. "Get away!" I shout.

He recoils with a hiss between his teeth and grabs my other wrist. "You are rather a fool. But I prefer my meals fighting anyway, and your tenderness is going to be a fresh bite." He presses me tightly to the stone wall, taking all leverage from me, and draws my right forearm to his lips.

I gulp a breath but don't anticipate that he will actually bite me. His teeth sink into my skin like I'm nothing but a soft peach, and I let out a shriek. Confusion and fear fuel it as much as the pain, but his teeth penetrate my skin so effortlessly there isn't much pain at first.

The noise makes him laugh and he runs his tongue across my wound, lapping at the blood. "Even better than I had hoped. You are filled with light. I knew the moment I saw that purple eye of yours. Yes. Perhaps I can regain some of that." He pins my wrists again above my head, crushing me against the stone wall. The pressure sends pain radiating through my bones. "I'm not sharing you with the others."

My pouch wiggles and Acorn pushes his way out. "You stay away!" he shouts and with all of his quills bristled, jabs his body into the evil fairy's chest.

He yelps and grabs Acorn, which only causes Acorn's quills to penetrate the skin on his hand. He growls and throws him, and I hear Acorn cry out as he slides across the floor, far away from us.

"No!" I try harder to get away. "You hurt him!"

He loops his finger in the collar of my under dress and pulls it down to expose the skin of my shoulder.

My heart thunders in my ears.

"Get off of me! Release me now!" I shout as loudly as I can. "You will have to deal with the prince and his guard if you don't release me immediately!" I thrash, my feet scraping feebly at the floor and wall, but he only adds pressure to my body, squeezing the air out of me. I have never felt more helpless.

Worse, the fairy is completely undeterred by my threats. Neither Kai nor Garrett is here, and I can't see any other being in the hallway.

When the creature sinks his fangs into my shoulder, I don't hold back and release the loudest scream I can muster. This causes him to bite a second time, but much harder and much deeper.

He growls. "I will give you a reason to scream, little girl." He slams his elbow against the side of my head.

Pain explodes in my ear and stars blind me. I feel myself drop to the floor and sense the weight of the fairy on my chest, his knee pinning my right wrist to the ground. When my vision comes back, the monster looms over me with my middle finger between his teeth. He is about to sink his teeth into my knuckle and undoubtedly dislodge my finger from its joint.

"No! Please!" I cry and struggle with all I have. My boots

scramble pathetically and I can't arch my back off of the floor. All of my efforts are futile. I'm like a fly caught in a web, and no amount of struggling will free me.

Pain sears through my finger and I cry out again.

I hear rushed footsteps, a shout, and then a thud as a human body slams into the fairy, tackling him off of me and to the ground.

A rush of adrenaline allows me to bolt upright, gulping in air, but fear freezes me in place.

Kai's large form is now on top of the fairy, slamming his fists into the creature's face. The fairy roars and swings his legs, getting one of them around Kai's waist to roll him. But I've watched Kai train with the other soldiers and know he doesn't need a weapon to gain the upper hand. He rolls with the movement, loops his arm through the fairy's, and gains the upper hand by pulling the fairy's back across his. He twists, pulling the fairy's shoulder over his own, and a sickening *pop* hits the air.

The fairy screams in agony as his shoulder is either broken or dislocated.

Kai kicks his feet against the wall at my side for leverage and flings himself back, once again on top of the fairy. He twists, grabs the creature by the head, and slams it against the stone floor. This stuns the fairy long enough for Kai to adjust his grip.

Garrett suddenly falls on his knees at my side and pulls my head into his chest. But I still hear the sound of the fairy's head striking the stone floor twice more, each with a grunt of effort from Kai.

And then all I hear is the two of them panting and Garrett's heartbeat in my ears.

"Is he dead?" Garrett asks softly, but his voice sounds so loud in my head.

"I think so."

Garrett moves his arm and Kai inspects my shoulder. The anger burning in his brown eyes slowly fades. He silently slides one arm beneath my legs, wraps the other around my back, and picks me up.

"Is she okay?" I hear Acorn ask.

"She will be. You were brave," Garrett replies. "Are you injured?"

"No. I'm fine."

I'm trembling like a leaf in Kai's arms.

He takes me directly to his cell, sits on his bed, and rests me in his lap. It is only then I realize that I'm crying and clutching so desperately to his vest and shirt that my knuckles are white. The pristine gold of his vest is now smeared red with my blood. Blood splatters his knuckles and the sleeve of his right arm.

"I've got you," he whispers comfortingly. "Breathe. There you go. Again. Slow. In through your nose, out through your mouth," he coaches.

My heart has finally released its grip on my throat. "He was going to eat me!" I shout.

Kai rests his cheek on top of my head and smooths my hair. "I wouldn't have let that happen."

Garrett steps forward, holding Acorn in his hands, and kneels. "How do I search in your pouch for medicine you need?"

"You reach in," Kai says gruffly.

Garrett glares at him. "She enchanted it so it's bigger on the inside."

"Not right now. Please," I beg.

Kai's grip on me tightens. "I'm sorry."

"We really need water to clean the wound properly," Garrett mutters. "We don't know what that dark fairy's teeth may have done."

"I'll find it!" Acorn scrambles into the pouch. Seconds later, he shoves the poultice out, along with the vial of pink healing liquid. "And I think this will work since we don't have water."

I grimace. "That's difficult to make and should be used in emergencies."

"I would say this is an emergency," Kai states, his tone edging on annoyance.

"I'm not broken," I counter sharply. "What if you get broken by that wolf next time? You can't tell me he didn't hurt you."

Kai shakes his head. "Garrett has a point about the fairy's saliva. Fairies are magical, and what if going bad made it poisonous or something?"

I can't deny that with the rush of adrenaline gone, my shoulder feels like it's on fire. Each breath sends sharp pain all the way down into my ribs, and I've only just managed to get *those* healed!

Garrett accepts the vial from Acorn and pops the cork. He says nothing as he holds it up to me, but I read the earnest insistence in his gaze.

"It's the only one I have," I try one more time. "I think we should try the poultice first."

Kai moves his hand to my knee, and his wedding band glints in the light. "I can help put it on."

Is it wrong if I let him help? "I can manage," I say weakly.

The fingers on his hand twitch into a fist, but he resists the urge to hold me in place. His other arm drops.

I climb off of his lap, hissing between my teeth, but turn. "Thank you for saving me. I thought he was going to . . ." My breath hitches.

Kai picks up my hand and kisses my palm. I can tell he wants to say something, but he doesn't. "I'll always be there for you, El," he whispers. "No matter what."

I want to believe him. My attention drifts to the wedding band on his finger. "Is your wedding even valid?" I ask. "Was it all just a farce?"

He follows my gaze and his brows furrow with thought. "According to our laws, we are married. Even if she's a fairy. Which only complicates everything now."

"What happened?" a voice demands.

I lift my gaze to see Tem with three waterskins draped over his arm. He's looking from me to the other two with his only eye.

"A fairy monster attacked her," Garrett explains. "Prince Kaison . . . stopped him."

"Ah. The dead hag in the hallway." He points his thumb over his shoulder. "They'll be questioning you about that."

Kai shrugs. "He should have kept his teeth and hands to himself."

"He bit you?" Tem reaches out. "May I?" I let him assess the bite mark on my finger, forearm, and finally move the collar of my nightgown to assess the deepest of the wounds. He clicks his tongue.

"What is a hag?" I ask.

"A fairy who loses their purity. Fairies are born of light. You understand this as a magic user."

I nod and in doing so draw pain up into my neck.

"Well, when fairies begin to entertain dark or evil thoughts, they begin to lose their light. Those who begin this path lose the color of their wings first. It is the only warning before they are entirely consumed and become hags. If you do not return to the light you were born from, you will become the darkness you created. You're going to need some medicine."

The alarm blares, alerting all prisoners to return to their cells.

"You wouldn't happen to have any sort of bandages to help her?" Garrett asks.

"I'll have to see if the guards allow me to get it and return to you. They're pretty strict on their time for the doors locking." He hands the men the waterskins. "They only fill it once a day, but they may be a little lenient, considering the injury."

Kai uncaps his without hesitation and holds it out to me. "Use mine to rinse the wound."

"Oi, you four! In your cells!" a fairy guard with yellow wings hollers from down the hall.

Tem puts on a dashing smile and turns to face him. "Ah, Malachi. It's good to see you. This young lady was attacked by one of the hags and has some wounds. Do you mind if I fetch some bandages for her?"

The fairy stops a safe distance away, his lips tight. Over his right shoulder is another fairy, this one with pink-red wings, who has his sword drawn.

"The men need to step into their cells," he finally responds. His attention locks on Kai and the blood on his clothing. "You'll be condemned for murdering one of us."

"It wasn't a fairy any longer," Kai replies coldly. "And I wouldn't have had to if it hadn't attacked Elowyn. She shouldn't even be here. Surely you are not the only one to notice she's the only female in this prison? We all know this puts her in significant danger."

I want to argue that I'm not fragile, that he taught me

how to fight, but I was completely useless against the dark fairy—or hag—just moments ago. If I had trained at a university, I might have been able to cast spells and actually put up a fight. What good is enchanting in a situation like that?

The fairy refocuses on Tem and nods. "I'll escort you personally." He extends an arm toward the cell I share with Garrett. "Go in."

Kai steps forward.

The fairy's eyes darken. "I said you to your cell. I have full permission to punish you if you disobey, whether or not you're Queen Genoa's prize."

"Queen?" Kai's brow twitches.

The fairy scoffs. "You are so oblivious."

Kai's jaw flexes.

"Kai, Garrett is with me," I say, not wanting him to be punished over something so foolish. He's already on thin ice with the dead hag. I'm also in too much pain to argue further.

He sucks a breath in through his nose and looks to me. "I'm sorry."

Garrett gestures to himself. "I'm pretty experienced in protecting others."

"You didn't keep her safe from the fairy, did you?" Kai's tone is cold.

Garrett snorts. "Because you shoved me to the ground as I was running."

The fairy arches his brow. "I really want to be celebrating with my family right now, but here I am trying to get a stubborn human to return to his cell before I have to beat him."

"Kai, just do as they say," I say with all the firmness I have left. I step away from him and into my cell.

Garrett follows.

The door clatters shut and the lock clicks in place.

I face Kai through the bars. "I've been fine for the past year. It's just one night."

Kai drops his gaze and turns to his own cell. I feel bad, but at the same time, we have each forged our paths.

"Humans." The fairies slip into their own language and their voices fade.

Garrett takes the waterskin Kai gave him and faces me. "I would have been there first. Hold your breath."

I look away as he pours the icy water across my shoulder. I gasp and somehow manage to resist the urge to pull away. Not only is it freezing, but it stings the moment it comes in contact with my open wounds.

Acorn climbs out and drops to the ground. "I'm never getting a normal day's sleep around here." He wraps around the jar of poultice and unscrews the lid.

Garrett steps in front of me and grasps my opposite arm. "Sit down. You're pale." With his help, I lower to the ground. He accepts the poultice from Acorn and dips his fingers in. "Will this sting?"

"A little, but only because of the pressure of actually applying it." I hold the shirt down. "I can do it."

He responds by pressing the poultice into the bite as gently as he can, spreading it in a thin layer. The off-white ointment changes to pink as it mixes with my blood. "Prince Kaison never should have sought you out after being turned into a frog. He should have gone to his father. Some other poor wizard or sorcerer should be caught up in this. Not you."

I refuse to look at him. "Well, I'm sorry you're stuck with a useless witch who can't even cast spells."

He lifts my chin with his finger. "That wasn't what I meant. You deserve to be taken care of, Elowyn. You deserve to be safe and protected. You deserve someone by your side, not stringing you along and playing with your heart when it's convenient for him."

"Kai isn't like that. You may know him as a soldier, but you don't know him the way I do." I pull my face away from his touch. "He came to me because he knew what happened was wrong and he didn't know who else to trust. I was happy to help him. Maybe I actually hoped for the chance to have him break off the wedding?"

Garrett rubs some more of the poultice into the wound on my arm. "It's not my place. I shouldn't say anything more."

The lock clicks and the door grinds open.

We both turn to see Tem enter. "I've got a whole basket

of supplies, which includes some ingredients so you can make more poultice. There are bandages as well. I recommend putting a leaf of goldtongue under your tongue to help with the pain." He shows me the plant he refers to. I've never seen it before and I wonder if it's specific to the fairy realm.

"This way, sir," the guard commands.

Tem steps back out. "Rest well. I'll see you at the break tomorrow morning."

Garrett returns to my side and pulls out one of the rolls of bandages. "You're going to have to hold your arm away from your body so I can properly wrap it. The bite is in a very inconvenient location, unfortunately."

I lift my arm and immediately grimace. "Mmm. Talk," I say. "I want to think about something else. You said you were an orphan? Do you have friends?"

"Yes. A good handful." Garrett slips the bandage under my arm. "One of them is a man named Robert. I think you would find him amusing. He's shorter than you and feisty. He's deceptively fast and can slip into the enemy's defenses without being spotted."

I rest my head on the wall. "He is a soldier?"

Garrett nods. "A good one too. Then there is Darnick, who is about five years older than I am and can beat anyone in a drinking contest."

"You drink?"

Garrett grins. "Every soldier does. Prince Kaison can

best most of us, but even he hasn't beaten Darnick."

"I'm pretty sure he's part dwarf," Kai adds from his cell.

My attention drifts to him. It's the first time Kai has spoken since we returned to our cells. The soldier life is a side of Kai I've never known. He won't speak about his war memories with me aside from where he went.

Garrett finishes wrapping the bandage and then tugs the bloody sleeve back up on top, though it's a bit futile considering how much it's stretched.

"Have you and Kai ever fought together?" I ask softly.

Garrett nods. "On more than one occasion."

"Are you friends?" I ask.

He hesitates. "Sort of," he eventually says. "It's not that kind of relationship. It's more of a duty to the throne." He drapes his cloak across me and leans his body against my good shoulder for some added warmth. "I would trust the prince with my life on any battlefield, and I would lay it down for him. I would like to believe he would do the same for me."

"I would," Kai replies. He sits with his back and head against the wall, and his knees are up so his arms are resting on them. "I'm sorry I dragged both of you into this," he whispers.

"You didn't know the full truth," Garrett says.

Kai's lips tug. "Yeah. Well. You're right. I should have gone to my father. He knew the truth and would have probably understood what was going on. Maybe he could have spoken with Genoa before we broke their binding."

"Maybe this is just one of those times fate is unavoidable," Garrett adds.

I feel my head drift to Garrett's shoulder and don't bother trying to sit back up. I'm overwhelmed by exhaustion.

Garrett helps shift me so I'm lying on the ground with my head in his lap. He drapes his cloak over me.

As much as I don't want it, I want it. I want to be held. I want *someone* to love me. And would it be so bad if it were an honorable soldier instead of a prince?

## Chapter Seventeen

Acorn bumps his nose against my hand. "I brought something for you."

"What?" I mumble.

"The fairy gave me clothes for you. It took me all night! I had to drag each piece the entire way. Do you know how much energy that took?"

I peel my eyes open and find I'm on my left side with my forearm aching. My right shoulder has a dull throb, and . . . Garrett's arm is wrapped around my stomach, holding me against his chest. His cloak is over the two of us and I think I might have actually slept.

His warmth seeps into me and I am grateful for it. His breath is soft, and with him sleeping, I can look over my shoulder and see him without feeling like I'm staring. The edges of his beard on his cheeks have filled out and are no longer carefully groomed, and his mustache is no longer curled. His brown hair is messy too. And I notice for the first time a light scar on the left side of his jaw.

Why do I keep letting my emotions run back to Kai when Garrett is right here? He has kept me safe and put up with my attitude, and he's funny. We're probably a better match that Kai and me. Maybe it's time to let Kai go.

"El?" Acorn speaks up.

"Hm?" I refocus my attention on him and the pile of clothes he's standing on. "Right. Clothes. Wait. The fairy gave these to you?"

He nods, rolls onto his side, and tucks his body together into a little ball. "I heard you talking to him yesterday. I wanted to adventure, because I'm hungry and there aren't worms coming out of the rocks, so I was trying to find something to eat. I saw him. He told me his name is Temarilian, that he is the missing king of the fairies, and that he had clothes for you."

I put my weight on my good arm and push up. Garrett's arm is heavy on my side, so I have to carefully lift it and set it against his own body. The cold nips at my exposed skin. "Wait, he's a king?"

"It took me all night to drag it all to you!" Acorn continues. "Do you know how difficult it is to run with something longer than you? And I didn't find anything to eat! Now I'm starving. Did you know there are rats as big as me? They told me I looked good and I prickled them."

I reach out and muffle a groan of pain when it explodes through my shoulder. I reach out with only my right hand and pick him up. "Acorn, what do you mean he is the king?"

He shrugs. "He's the king. The orb told me to go and find him. That he's good."

"Is everything okay?" Garrett asks, voice heavy with

sleep. When I look at him, he's propped up on his elbow.

"Acorn brought me clothes." I rise up onto my knees and turn back to the hedgehog. "The orb talks to you?"

He licks his hands and cleans his face. "Yes. It told me the fairy was going to eat you so I had to save you."

"Hm. I wonder why it talks to you." I pick up the trousers. They're brown and in perfect shape. Tem wouldn't have extra clothes, in pristine condition, inside of a prison if he weren't someone important. They're going to do much better keeping my legs warm, and my body overall. "Has it told you why it talks to you?"

Acorn scrunches up. "It likes me. It said something about being connected to you, and Kai to you, and you to Kai. I wasn't paying attention. I'm sleeping now. Good day."

"It's connected to us? What do you mean?"

"I'm sleeping. You ask it," he mutters.

"Acorn. Acorn?"

He ignores me.

I roll my eyes and set him into the pouch. "Stubborn thing."

Garret rolls onto his back and places an arm under his head. His muscles bulge against his shirt. How have I not noticed that? "How long have you had him?"

"A few years."

"He's amusing." He smiles.

I manage to get to my feet without hurting my shoulder. "Garrett, Acorn said Tem is a king. Do you think he could be?"

He raises his eyebrow. "Huh. I mean, that explains why the prisoners and soldiers respect him. Do you need some help?" He doesn't wait for me to answer before he's rolled up to his knees.

My first reaction is to refuse his help. It's what I would normally do—be stubborn and fight through the pain in order to appear independent. But just leaning over to pick up the pants sent pain burning through my shoulder. If I want to get over Kai, I may as well accept Garrett's assistance.

"I would appreciate the help," I reply.

"Let's get your boots off first." He carefully grasps my bare calf, and the heat of his hand rushes blood and heat through my body. I nearly lose my balance and have to grab his head to avoid tipping over. He chuckles.

My heart skips and I can feel my cheeks flush. "Sorry."

"Don't worry about it." He remains steady as he bunches the pant legs so I can easily step into the holes. His thumbs glide up my legs as he helps me pull them up, sending even more tingles through me.

Kai has held me before. We have held hands, and he even kissed my forehead yesterday. But no one has ever been *this* close to me.

I grab the waist of the pants when they're at my knees, but bolts of pain etch through my shoulder like the pain carving deep veins through my arm. Garrett shifts his hands to the front, allowing me to grasp the back so I can pull them up and over my bum. I also notice how he is looking away while doing so, allowing me privacy even though my nightgown hangs down over the front.

"They're up," I say softly.

He nods, drops his hands, and collects the shirt and his cloak.

My hands are trembling as I button the pants, and not from the cold.

"I'll hold up my cloak for some privacy. Let me know if you need help with the shirt. You may want to start by putting your right arm in first." He holds up the cloak and closes his eyes. His facial hair is growing on me.

I chew my bottom lip. I accept the shirt from him and glance at the bandage on my shoulder. It's soaked with blood. "Do we have any more bandages?"

Garrett lowers the cloak and looks at my shoulder. He frowns before returning to the basket Tem gave us to get the last bundle of bandages. "We've got this and the last of your poultice. As for your . . ." He pauses and then lifts up the vial of healing liquid I didn't drink. "Elowyn."

"Okay! I'll drink a little."

"Or all of it."

"I don't think my shoulder is that bad."

He frowns. "Let's take off your dress so I can wrap it a little better. You can hold my cloak as a shield." He holds it out. "Are you all right if I rip your dress to make it easier to pull off?"

I feel my cheeks flush with heat and avert my gaze. "It's an under dress, and it's now stained with blood. I don't care if you shred it, just as long as it doesn't hurt."

I know Garrett will be polite and keep me modest, so I accept his cloak. He helps me tuck it under my right arm so I can wrap it around the upper part of my body, and then he grabs the collar of my nightgown and easily tears the thin fabric.

This would be intimate were it not for the bandage soaked well through with my blood. It's also slipped so it's barely on, as he was only able to loop it under my armpit. One of the bites is half visible.

I understand now why it feels that something is digging into me. Black veins stretch out from the wound like the spiny legs of a black widow spider. "I . . . I think I'll drink that healing liquid." My voice feels so small.

"Drink all of it. And we need Tem to take a look." He gives me the vial and I drink it as he massages the last of the poultice into the bite marks before wrapping the bandage under my armpit and then around my chest for some added stability.

My stomach knots. Kai was the one who saved me. Would I feel differently about this moment if Garrett had reached me first? Would I feel differently if Kai weren't married? I shake my head. Of course. Everything would be different if anything were different.

"I'll close my eyes and hold the cloak up at the door so no one can look in," Garrett says, looking away. "Get the shirt on. Tell me if I can help."

I nod silently.

He keeps his gaze away as he takes the cloak from me and goes to the cell door to hold it up.

Once my nightgown is off, cold bites so hard I'm surprised I can't see my breath. I guide my injured arm into one of the long sleeves first so I don't have to twist my shoulder, then my other arm. Getting it over my head makes me hiss, but I don't have to raise my shoulder much. I instantly feel warmer.

"Can you help me get my boots back on?" I ask.

"Yes." He drapes his cloak back over his shoulders and takes me in with his eyes. "Do you feel a little better?"

I nod. "Much, thank you."

"There has to be some sort of medical bay. We have those in our prisons." Like before, he takes my leg but this time guides my foot into my shoes. "You need some repairs." He pokes his fingers into the hole by my pinky toe.

"I know." I sigh. "I just haven't done it yet."

A squeaking wheel and metal rattling echoes down the hall. There's a loud clang, and Garrett quickly turns to face the door.

I look over to see a fairy crouch and slide two trays of food under it. The fairy has a broken left wing, which has faded blue tones while the other is still vibrant.

"Thank you," Garrett says before I can. He steps over me to retrieve the food.

"Don't know how tolerable it is," the fairy replies.

Garrett offers a slight smile. "Food is food." He crosses over to me and holds out a tray. "I recommend you eat, even if it doesn't taste good. We don't know what their feeding schedule is here and you need whatever energy you can get."

I accept the tray and lift my lip in disgust. It's a blob of gray with some sort of lumps in it. "You want me to eat this?"

Garrett has seated himself near the door and already has his spoon in his hand. "Like I said, we need whatever energy we can get."

"Unless they've poisoned it." I raise my brows at him.

He shrugs. "We have no way of knowing." But he stares at the poor excuse for food on his tray. "They wouldn't kill us."

"You have such confidence in strangers." I sit across from him.

"I understand the dynamics of powerful people." He scoops a spoonful and deposits it in his mouth. His lips tug down and he shrugs one shoulder. "Not the worst I've had, surprisingly."

I glance over at Kai's cell for the first time that morning. I haven't wanted to. I can see his silhouette, sitting on the floor of his cell against the bars of the far walls. The way the light comes in from behind shields his face in shadow, but he must have been watching everything. Unless he's sleeping sitting up.

"Did you sleep?" I call to him.

"About as well as a flea on a frog."

I smile because fleas can't live on frogs. It's a common saying, but funnier considering he was a frog just yesterday. I let my attention drift back to my food, but my stomach feels heavy already and I don't want to eat.

Garrett touches my knee.

I acknowledge him with my eyes.

The edge of his lip tugs sadly. "I know you care for him. He's always loved you. It's annoying how much he talks about you." He looks at his food. "I understand why now."

I shake my head immediately. "It's too late. He's married. I guess that's what hurts the most. No matter what . . . I can't have him."

Garrett leans his back against the wall. "It's hard losing someone you love."

"You've been in a relationship before?" I look him up and down.

"What, I can't love?" He smiles. "Yes. She was a seamstress and we tried to make it work."

"But?" I shove a spoonful of slop into my mouth and immediately gag at the texture. It's more sticky and thick than oatmeal with pieces of some sort of nut in it. Walnut perhaps? No. More like pecan. Garrett is right, it's not awful. But the texture is.

He shrugs. "I had nothing to offer her family. Her father refused to let us be together, and she found someone else."

"Not so different than me, hm?" I sigh and slowly return to eating.

"You aren't alone, Elowyn." I like the way he says my name.

The broken-winged fairy returns to collect our bowls. Mine is still half-full, but I can't stomach any more.

Almost as soon as he's gone, the alarm for the doors unlocking sounds. Is it already time for the morning break? Did we sleep that long?

With Garrett closest to the door, he steps out first, but I am quick to follow behind. The longer I'm away from Kai, the more I can't help but feel like I want to be with him. There are bags under his eyes as he joins us in the hall.

"How is your shoulder?" he asks.

"It seems infected," I reply and glance down at it, though he can't see through the bandages.

"It looks like it's branching out too," Garrett adds.

Kai focuses his attention on Garrett. "How bad?"

I briefly catch a glimpse of Garrett shaking his head and my stomach drops. It must be bad. These two soldiers have undoubtedly seen a lot of injuries, and he doesn't want to tell me out loud how significant it is.

"Good morning, human trio!" Tem greets the instant we are outside, his attitude upbeat and far more energetic than I feel this morning. "Ah! Acorn succeeded in delivering your clothes. How do you feel?"

"Warmer," I respond. "But we're concerned about the injury."

Garrett scratches his scruff. "Is there a hospital bay where we can change the bandages out and get medicine?"

Tem grimaces. "Ah, well, I'm afraid not. This place is a prison to stay until you die. They don't care how that happens."

"Yet you clearly have some sway with the soldiers," Kai points out.

Garrett leans his head to Kai's ear. "That's because he's the fairy king."

Kai's eyes widen.

As do Tem's. And then Tem sighs and glances at me. "Acorn?"

"He's never been very good at keeping secrets," I admit.

Tem rubs the back of his neck. "Not that it really matters. Not with you three. In spite of my previous rank, Genoa has removed me from my throne. I cannot force the soldiers to give you bandages or medicine. What I gave you last night was a courtesy, but they cannot show favorites to anyone, even if I used to be their king."

"Do we have any chance of getting out of here?" Kai asks.

Tem shakes his head. "Possibly, but we must be very cautious." He pauses and looks over his shoulder to see a handful of the evil fairies approach us.

"The prince is a murderer!" a hag snarls, pointing with a crooked finger in his direction. "He killed one of us!"

"Because that hag attacked her and tried to eat her flesh," Kai replies calmly. "Do I have no right to protect her?"

"Did you have to kill him?" the other argues.

Three more head our direction.

Tem clears his throat softly. "Return to whatever you were doing. Let the humans be. Genoa claims dominion over them."

One growls. "For now."

"Do you really want to add more injury to them and risk her wrath?" Tem folds his arms over his chest.

The group disbands and I let out my breath, knowing this likely won't be the last time we encounter them. We need to get out of here. And fast.

## Chapter Eighteen

"You three certainly attract a lot of attention." Tem rests his hands on his hips and faces us. "I don't know when Genoa is planning on arriving today to collect you." Tem steps so close to Kai, Garrett actually puts his hand on the fairy's chest. Tem shakes his head, voice low. "Acorn told me about the orb you have. You have one of the Orbs of Olwar."

"Orbs of Olwar?" I raise my brow. We all exchange brief glances of confusion.

"Come with me on a walk. We need to get away from mischievous ears." He tilts his head toward the crowd, steps back, puts on his easy smile, and begins walking around the perimeter of the yard, but toward the exit.

"Do we trust him?" Garrett asks.

"Acorn does," I comment. "He's a hard sell."

Tem turns his head so his one eye can see us. "We don't have time for me to prove anything."

Kai shrugs in a way that says, "*He has a point.*"

We stop at a cell on the opposite side of the entrance from where ours are. Tem's cell is far more elaborate and removes all doubt that he is someone important. He has a real bed, a chest at the foot of it, a wardrobe, and even a chair and small bookshelf.

"Lay the orb on my bed," he says.

I hesitate, but the orb begins to grow hot against my leg. *It is safe,* a voice coaxes through my mind.

Carefully, I open the pouch and allow the golden ball to roll out. My heart is racing. Acorn said the ball spoke to him, but this is my first time hearing it. There is something disconcerting about a voice in my head. I swallow down my discomfort.

"What is an Orb of Olwar?" I ask.

Tem's smile saddens. "No one exactly knows where they came from or how they were formed. There are two in existence, as far as we know. They are sentient and have been part of our history for centuries."

"What do they do?" Kai asks.

Tem reaches out and places his hand on the orb, then runs his thumb across the surface. I read sadness in every movement. "They bring power to the king and queen, but only if they are truly in love. It grants us the ability to share one another's power."

"Why does this make you sad?" I ask.

"Because it is no longer linked to me," he whispers. Tears brim his eyes. "She no longer loves me." Tem clears his throat and straightens. "We have little time, if any. All we have to do is sneak out through one of the guard entrances and then get back to your realm through one of the unlocked fairy portals."

"You make it sound easy," Garrett says flatly.

Tem shrugs. "The hardest part is going to be getting out of the prison."

I point my thumb behind me. "I don't know if you've noticed, but this place seems pretty impenetrable."

This earns a chuckle from Kai.

"Because I am who I am," Tem starts, "I know where all of the exits are and which one will be the easiest for us to escape through." He turns all attention to me. "Does your purple eye indicate that you are a human magic wielder?"

I nod. "You know about that?"

"Yes. I've met quite a few humans. What do you know about enchanting?"

I smile. "That happens to be my strongest form of magic."

"Then we have a way to escape." His eye lights up and he rubs his hands with excitement.

"And that would be?" I ask.

"We need you to enchant something to make us shrink. Can you do that?"

I almost laugh because I've used that enchantment multiple times, including the liquid used to make the troll shrink, and practically have it memorized. I smile widely. "I can."

He winks. "Smart girl."

I dig into my pouch to fish out the grimoire and sit on the edge of the bed to leaf through the pages. I need a reminder of the rune's shape. In sitting on the bed, however, the orb rolls and bumps against me.

*Trust in your own knowledge.* The voice is masculine and somehow close and distant at the same time, like an echo. It somewhat resembles Kai's voice, and I feel warmth fill me.

I look around.

"What?" Kai steps close.

"Ah. Yes." Tem clears his throat. "I forgot to mention there is a mental connection with the orbs. They're sentient, remember?"

I blink and place my hand on my racing heart. "It spoke to me."

"Yes. They do that." Tem smiles softly.

I glance up at Kai and then back down at the ball on the bed. I reach down and pick it up. Its energy is warm. "Why does it speak to me, though?"

*You know what the rune looks like. You know how to use it. Stop second-guessing yourself and cast the spell.*

"Can't you just transfer us out of here with magic or something?" I ask it.

*You must find your own way. The guard is coming.*

I slip the orb into the pouch and throw it over my shoulder. "We should go," I say. "The guards are coming and we can't get caught."

Garrett is the first to leave the cell, followed by Kai and me. Tem takes up the rear.

The fairy guard, who has bright green wings, eyes us. "You have a chance to be outside and you're in here?"

"It's safer than walking laps around the monsters," Kai points out.

"Especially since they want to kill him for the hag," Garrett chimes in.

Kai's brow twitches. "I wasn't going to add that part."

The fairy steps to the side and gestures, hand on his sword. "There are some creatures who cannot enter the light. They're more dangerous than a hag. I recommend you go where we can keep a better eye on you."

"For our own safety?" Kai asks.

"Something like that," he replies flatly.

"Thank you for the warning," I say, dragging Kai forward. "We'll go back outside."

Tem bows his head. "Thank you, Rendesh."

Rendesh gives a wisp of a smile before continuing down the hall.

"We are in luck," Tem says the instant we are around the corner. "Rendesh is forever loyal to me. I took him in after his father was killed, shortly before being put here. If he sees us during the escape, he isn't going to turn on me."

Once outside, I walk a small square, keeping an eye on the crowd without appearing to do so, though I imagine I'm failing miserably. We've been given a bit of space, but they seem more on edge than they did yesterday and I have an itch at the back of my mind they are planning something.

Hopefully we can escape before anything worse happens.

"Will we even have a chance to escape in daylight?" I mutter under my breath.

"I think Acorn is rubbing off on you," Garrett says. He's walking back and forth just beyond my square.

Kai is slumped against the wall, arms folded across his chest, head down. He really must not have slept last night to be asleep right now. Though the sun is definitely warm and calming.

I smile as I make eye contact with Garrett and stop when we meet.

He pauses and eyes me. "Are you okay?"

I bite my lip. "I feel like I need to be honest about Kai," I whisper.

He holds up his hand. "I know your heart belongs to him. Even though you're mad at him, you have deep feelings I don't know if anyone can fill."

I look down at my feet.

"He cares just as deeply. You should have seen him after he was given the order to arrest you or your mother. He met with her."

My eyes widen and my breath hitches. "What?" I say it a bit louder than intended and Kai's eyes fly open.

"He spoke with her before he arrested her," Garrett repeats, his back to Kai and unaware the prince has woken. "He told her about his father's order and how he didn't know what to do. He was certain you would never forgive him if he arrested her, but he couldn't put you in prison. He begged her for help. Your mother made the decision for him."

Tears fill my eyes and I look past Garrett. Kai is now standing. "Why didn't you tell me?"

Garrett turns and steps back. When Kai doesn't immediately answer, Garrett does for him. "He didn't want you mad at her."

Kai licks his lip. "It made more sense at the time to me. I didn't think that you would stay mad at me so long and end up completely alone. Your mother said she left a letter for you."

Guilt washes over me. I've only ever read the first paragraph, where she tells me she will be fine in prison and that I should keep practicing magic and take care of the homestead. I couldn't bear to read the rest.

My loneliness is entirely my fault.

Kai getting married was because I pushed him away.

I turn away, but Kai wraps his arms around me from behind and pulls me against his chest. "Don't be angry with yourself. There's so much you didn't know."

"How can I not hate myself?" I whisper.

He cradles my arms and leans his cheek against mine. "You were surviving. Everyone reacts to situations differently, and I cannot fault you for trying to make it through each day."

"Look where that's gotten us." My voice cracks.

"Because of me we're in a prison. Worse, you're now stuck with a fairy as a wife."

"Shh. There isn't anything I wouldn't do to keep you safe, even if it meant pushing you away."

I turn to face him and see his eyes brimming with tears. "I'm sorry for how I've treated you."

"I am sorry too. I should have involved you in that conversation." He places his hand on my jaw and rubs his thumb across my cheekbone. "But there are too many 'should have' situations. We cannot change the past."

I nod. We have to figure out how to move forward from here. But I'm not ready to replace Kai yet. I'm not ready to let anyone else take his place in my heart.

The temperature drops around us, and everyone, including the other prisoners, looks around for the source.

Kai drags me behind him and Garrett steps in front of the prince. I think we all know why the atmosphere has become cold, and it is only confirmed when a shadow descends from above.

Genoa lands in the center of the space. Her skin is pale beneath the sunlight and the color of her wings is more pastel than I recall. "My good creatures. I've come to collect my prize. I must show him to the people before we return to claim his kingdom as ours. And then none of you will need to be in this wretched place any longer."

From the corner of my vision, I notice Tem back up and slip into the crowd, disappearing into their numbers.

Genoa turns and holds her hand out toward us, eyes locked on Kai. "Come, my husband."

Kai places his hand on Garrett's shoulder and nudges him out of the way. "Keep your vow. Get Elowyn out of here," he whispers. "Go with Tem. Keep her safe."

"Your Highness," he objects.

Kai has sacrificed everything for me.

He let me go to change the laws so I can follow my dreams.

I may not know war magic. I may not know how to cast fireballs and call upon lightning. But I know nature. I know plants. I have leaned on the goodness of nature my entire life.

I run forward and cut in front of Kai, making him bump into me.

"El, what are you doing?" he whispers.

"You aren't taking him!" I shout at the fairy sorceress. "You've destroyed enough. You can't have him too."

Genoa grins. "You're going to challenge me, little witch?"

"El, don't be foolish," Kai warns. He puts his hand on my hip and tries to push me aside.

I shove against him and retake my place as his shield. "You're a fairy and belong in your realm. Kai belongs on the throne you placed him on."

"He does. With me at his side." Her grin falls. "You are pestering me, child."

"Can we come to no other arrangement?" I ask. "His father made a vow with you, which has now been fulfilled. You know this means Kai can make a new treaty with you in order to benefit both of our races."

Genoa tilts her head, her blonde hair cascading down over her shoulder when she does so. "And what arrangement do you want that to be?"

I have no idea. I am rattling off whatever . . . whatever the orb is speaking to me. The orb is speaking *through* me. I didn't realize until this moment that the orb's voice fills my head. "A peace treaty. Your people can come and go through the human realm as they please. Laws regarding the regulation of magic will be reconsidered so fairies cannot be punished for simply living. Kai rules his throne, King Tem rules his."

Her brow twitches. "Tem? Temarilian?" She blinks, like she hasn't heard the name in ages. Her eyes darken. "Or I can do what I wish. Come, Prince Kaison. Before I tear her apart and feed her to my pets."

Kai grips my wrist and pushes me backward and against Garrett, no matter how hard my feet fight against him. His jaw is clenched, his lips tight, his eyes stern. "You stay with him."

Garrett grabs onto me to stop me from running after Kai again.

My fingers tingle with the familiar sensation of magical energy. I am not going to let Kai silently walk away from me into a future he cannot control when he has been a bargaining chip his entire life.

"*Etch na frier!*" I say.

The ground trembles.

Genoa's gaze snaps to me and Kai looks over his shoulder as the trembling grows into an earthquake so immense the prisoners begin to run.

"What are you doing?" Garrett demands.

The roots of the ancient tree in which we are imprisoned claw through layers of soil and penetrate through the stone floor that has been built to suppress them. I don't know how I understand, but the tree is as ancient as the fairy world and has been polluted with magic in an attempt to retain the prisoners. That is the magic I call to, but through that magic to the tree itself.

Genoa turns in a circle as the roots spring up and grapple at her—and any living thing running away. A crack echoes and forms alone one of the far walls. "You think you can intimidate me with a little bit of magic?" She scoffs and reaches her hand out toward Kai. A shadowy hand shoots forth, grasps him around the neck, and drags him to her. "I gave you a chance to let him go willingly."

"I'm not letting him go!" Strength fills me, exploding in my chest, and I step away from Garrett. I reach for the tree, for the earth, for the air. "*Altech er undin! Etch na frier!*"

"Elowyn, stop!" Garrett shouts. "You don't know what you're doing!"

A root wraps around Genoa's ankle.

Garrett grabs onto my arm. "You're destroying the prison and putting our lives in danger!"

Genoa holds Kai with one hand and her glare bores into me. "He will die because of you. Is that what you want?"

Kai's feet kick and his hands grapple at Genoa's grip.

Fear seizes my air and I drop my hands. She's killing him. The shaking of the earth fades and dirt crumbles from the broken walls.

"You'll never see him again. Nizra!" she shouts. She beats her wings with force enough to kick up the dirt around us, blinding me.

I shield my face with my arm and feel Garrett hold me.

When the wind stops, I look around at the devastation I caused.

"We aren't escaping now," Garrett mutters, looking up in the direction Genoa has taken Kai.

My gaze lingers on their shapes until I can no longer see them. "You can stay if you want. I'm getting out of here." I begin walking over the lumps of roots bulging from the ground.

"And how do you plan on doing that?" Garrett chases after me.

"I don't know yet!"

Tem rushes over. "Now would be the most opportune moment to take advantage of the chaos to escape."

"Won't the guards be on higher alert?" Garrett asks.

"You're not as much of a threat as the others. Well, *you* aren't. *She* is. Regardless, we have a window of opportunity." He nudges us toward the hallway. "We won't have time to wait for you to cast spells to allow discretion. Do you know how to unlock doors?"

We step into the darkness, but two fairy guards land behind us, grasping my arms instantly. They say nothing before they pull my arms behind me and clamp cold metal onto my wrists. One of them is the soldier Tem mentioned earlier, Rendesh.

Garrett wheels, but Tem snatches his wrist before he does something he won't be able to take back. "Let her go!"

"She is a danger and will be treated as one," the unknown soldier replies.

"Where will you take her?" Tem asks, holding Garrett back.

Rendesh steps forward, drawing me with him. "To the dark cell. She will be safest there." He nods and steps past them, forcing me along.

I make eye contact with Garrett.

"She will be safe," Tem insists. "Don't worry, Elowyn."

I struggle to swallow.

A dull throb aches across the back of my head. The chains burn. Pain shoots through my shoulder. Fairy guards fill the hallway, ushering prisoners to their respective cells. I didn't even know there were so many fairy guards or where they came from. I am taken straight down the hall where

Tem's cell is, all the way until it ends at a guard door protected with a magical rune. The last cell on the right has a solid, heavy door. This is the cell Rendesh unlocks and slides open.

"You're making me stay in here?" I ask.

Rendesh removes my pouch. "I have no choice."

"You can't take that! That has my belongings! My property!"

The second soldier pushes me into the cell.

"My hedgehog is in there! He'll be concerned."

"We will take care of him," Rendesh says. They close the door and lock it.

I sink to my knees, struggling for breath as panic sucks the air from my lungs. I'm alone in a dark cell, the only light coming from beneath the door, and it's freezing. The more I shiver, the more my shoulder hurts. I don't even have Acorn for company.

What would Kai do in this situation?

Magic. I have magic.

Garrett may believe I am a danger, and he's right that I don't know what I'm doing, but Kai has always told me I have more inside of myself than I'm willing to admit. If he's willing to fight for me, I have to be willing to fight for him.

But when I try and access my magic . . . it's not there. There is a dark hole in the middle of my chest. How am I going to get out of this now?

## Chapter Nineteen

A strange sound slips under the door of my cell, the sound of metal scraping on stone. Or stone scraping on metal. Maybe someone is sharpening a weapon? I have no idea how much time has passed. The second alarm hasn't sounded, but they may have chosen to keep all prisoners locked away to repair the damage I caused. My arms ache from being forced behind my back, so it must be hours I've been here.

Acorn's little grunts reach me.

I blink and lean as far as I can to try to see under the door, but if I lie down I don't think I'll be able to get up.

Finally, his spiky body obscures the light and he wedges himself through the gap. He breathes hard and plops down flat on his belly like he's just climbed the largest mountain of his life.

"I'm so relieved to see you!" I scoot to him. "Are you okay? They didn't hurt you?"

"No." He blinks. "You've been in here for hours and you haven't escaped the chains yet? Muddy slugs, El!"

I scowl at him. "How do you expect me to escape?"

"You have magic, obviously."

I sink my shoulder against the wall. "I don't know what spell to use."

"You don't have an unlock spell?" he asks.

"Not memorized! I've never been locked out of anywhere and needed it. I don't have my grimoire, I don't have my mother, I don't know how to do this!" I don't mean to take it out on Acorn, but his pressing pessimism isn't helping right now when I'm in pain and stuck away from everyone and everything I know.

Acorn trots over and rests his little hands on my knee. "You don't need to be scared, El. I'm here. I can help. You know how to change an object into something else. You've done that before. Just make your chains worms and I can eat them!"

I can't help but laugh a little.

He rubs his face on me in a comforting gesture.

I remember a few of the words, but as soon as I say the first word electricity shoots through the chains and I cry out.

"What happened?" Acorn asks. He spins around in a circle.

I bite my bottom lip so hard I wonder if I've pierced it. "They must be enchanted to stop magic users from accessing their powers." I suck a breath and swallow hard.

"Hm. This isn't right." Acorn huffs. "Just know it's hard being your hero all the time." He turns away and scampers back through the hole he's entered.

"Acorn, where are you going? Acorn!"

Worry grips my chest and I scoot closer to the door. There's nothing I can do to help him. I feebly twist against the chains, but they still hold. Seconds tick by followed by agonizingly long minutes. Has it been an hour? Where is Acorn?

I lick my lips, my bottom lip now tender, and scoot my knees up to my chest. I may be able to step through the chains and get my wrists in front of me. When I struggle to step through, my shoulder explodes and I bite back another cry of pain.

Tears fill my eyes and I let my legs fall back down to the ground without any level of success.

The soft clattering of metal grinding on stone sounds softly from beneath the door. I suck in my breath, concerned it could be a soldier or something worse.

"You owe me lots of popping bugs," Acorn grunts. He grumbles under his breath as he wedges himself back through the hole.

"Acorn, what did you do?" I whisper.

"Relax. I told them I wanted more bugs." He breaks through, turns, and drags himself backwards, this time dragging with him a ring of keys. He drops them and beams at me. "They made it easy."

"Acorn. You're brilliant." I smile.

He drags them over, trotting happily. "The tiny one is for your chains." He finds the small key and wedges it into the manacle on my left wrist. "As much as I love adventures, as you know, I think I'm ready to go home and not move from your pillow for a month."

I chuckle. "That sounds wonderful. I'll bring you every bug I can find."

The lock clicks and the manacle falls. I groan as I pull my arm forward. My shoulder aches horribly and I bite my bottom lip. I'm grateful for the darkness of my cell, because I don't want to see what the hag's bite has done to my shoulder.

Acorn nudges the keys to me. "Let's get out of here and go home."

I take the keys, but don't immediately stand. "We don't have a plan. I might be able to unlock their doors with these keys, but then what? We can't just walk past the guards without drawing attention. And not only do I now have to get back to Garrett, we have to then find our way out of this prison." My throat feels tight.

Acorn places his hands on my boot. "Elowyn, you're too brave to be saying this. This isn't you."

I close my eyes. "I'm exhausted," I admit. "I hurt. I'm terrified of what has happened with Kai, and there is so much that can go wrong."

"All you have to do is shrink yourself and the other two, I carry you back through this hall, and we get out through the soldier room. They're exhausted from getting the prisoners put away and are resting. Only a few are doing their rounds tonight."

I look down at him. "You had a conversation with them?"

"What do you think took me so long?" He grins. "They fed me too. They have the most delicious beetles with purple shells and when you bite into them, they pop!"

I shudder. "Eww. Acorn, I don't want to know." I unlock my door and bite my bottom lip as I slowly and carefully slide the door open. The rollers grumble above, but I manage to keep it rather muted by moving slowly and methodically.

With a gap just wide enough for me to slip through, I scoop up Acorn, grasp the keys so they don't jingle, and run down the hall.

The first cell I reach is Tem's, and I say nothing as I begin searching the keys for the one to his cell. The ring has five large keys, two enormous keys, and seven or eight regular-sized keys. I find that the same key that unlocked my cell unlocks Tem's. I wonder if each key is a master key for each floor of the prison? And I don't want to know what the massive keys might be for.

"Tem!" I whisper as I approach his bed.

He instantly sits up. The light from the back wall of bars shines in and I can see him smile. "You're brilliant."

"It was Acorn." I hand Tem the keys. "Go and get Garrett. I'll make the rune to shrink us and we'll get out of here."

Tem climbs out of the bed, slips on his boots, and takes

the keys from me.

I take a moment to scan Tem's cell for something that will hold the enchantment long enough for all three of us to transform. An ordinary rock won't work. It might turn all three of us, but the enchantment may only last long enough for us to get to the door. I could enchant three separate rocks and that would last longer.

But not as long as the chunk of tree branch I notice on one of Tem's shelves. It doesn't matter that it's part of a tree. It was once a living, thriving thing with energy much different than cold stone. And when I touch the bark I immediately recognize the energy as that of the very tree in which we are trapped.

"Perfect!" I drop to my knees and trace the rune with two of my fingers on the ground, etching the symbol in the thin layer of dust.

Acorn wiggles from my hand and rolls up on his back to watch.

I mutter the words in my mind until I like how I'm pronouncing *ezdna*. Although I long for the familiarity of my mother's grimoire so I can triple-check that my drawing is correct, I don't have it and I'm going to have to trust in myself. I draw in a breath through my nose and slowly let it out through my lips. I repeat this as I close my eyes and center my magic inside of myself.

I hear the men's footsteps behind me and know it's them because I hear Tem whisper, "Don't interrupt her."

I feel the familiar tingle of magic from my fingertips to my tongue and toes. Slowly, I open my eyes.

"*Re hume, re ezdna, let ruendin.*" As I speak the enchantment, I trace the same rune symbol in the air. My magic, in a beautiful violet hue, forms the rune in the air. It crackles softly, like the popping of a candle. I place my hands on the piece of wood directly and repeat the enchantment. "*Re hume, re ezdna, let ruendin.*" I reach my right hand out, pluck the rune from the air, and press it against the rough surface. The rune etches into it, spreading across and intertwining with the ridges of the bark.

"Well?" Garrett asks carefully.

I smile. "Are you ready to go home?"

Garrett steps forward. "I'll go first."

Acorn laughs. "You're going to let her experiment on you?"

He shrugs. "I wouldn't trust anyone else."

"I would."

I roll my eyes. "You're such a pessimist."

He unrolls and gets to his feet. "Last time you tried to shrink something, you made a spruce tree the size of a weed."

"That was a spell, not an enchantment! They are different," I argue. "I managed to shrink that troll, didn't I?"

Garrett steps forward and touches the piece of wood with his hand. Immediately, he shrinks from over six feet to just a couple of inches at best. Tem follows, and I am the last one to touch the wood.

Electricity shoots through me and I feel like I've been dragged beneath water as the air is sucked from my lungs. I stumble and nearly fall, but Garrett is right there and catches me.

"Breathe," he says. "It's a bit shocking isn't it?"

I nod. "It was strange."

"Okay, everyone! Hop on!" Acorn wiggles his belly down on the floor to make it easier for us.

"I can't imagine this is going to be terribly comfortable for any of us," Garrett comments.

"I get to fly," Tem says with a smile.

With Garrett's help, I get on Acorn's back, and we exit the cell. I hold onto Acorn's quills and try to hold on the best I can, but this is nothing like riding a horse or donkey.

We could have easily run the distance to the guard's door in our full size. But being small enough to ride a hedgehog adds a significant amount of time, even if Acorn is running full speed.

Acorn gasps and skids, trying to dig his claws into the stone to make himself stop. To my right I see a rat bolting out from a hole, headed straight for us.

"Don't stop!" Garrett commands. "And I'm sorry."

"For what?" I ask.

Acorn yelps as Garrett drops down from his back, holding one of Acorn's quills in his hands like a sword. "That hurt!"

"Run!" Garrett shouts.

Acorn launches forward, dodging the rat's long teeth that snap at—and barely miss—my arm. Garrett swats the rat's nose with the quill, leaving a gash.

The rat shrieks. "You dare attack me?" It wheels on Garrett.

"We can't leave him behind!" I argue with Acorn.

"He told me to run, so I did!"

"Well, stop!" I order.

"No!"

Instead of continuing to argue with my terrified friend, I drop down from his back too. Only, I'm far less graceful, and when I land, my momentum carries me into a tumble. I manage to get to my feet and see Garrett now pointing the quill at three large rats, all snapping at him.

Tem lands on the ground at his side and blows a handful of dust in their faces.

The rats sneeze and one of them launches forward blindly, managing to swat Garrett's arm. I don't think he anticipated the force of the blow, because he hits the stone with a grunt.

"I don't know how well this is going to work." Tem loops his arms under Garrett's, lifting him up as his wings beat frantically to lift them both.

"I can run faster than this!" Garrett objects.

"Running isn't the aim right now," Tem states.

A rat jumps at them, missing Garrett's legs only because

he swings them out of the way, but in doing so he causes Tem to tilt sharply and nearly crash them both into a wall.

I know the rune for wind. I know the words and how to draw the symbol. I don't have time to find something to enchant and then throw it at the rats. I'm going to have to use the spell.

Holding both hands straight out with palms open, I say, "*Etch en wundar!*" Is it *wundar* or *wundur*? But I've already spoken the words of the spell and it's too late to be second-guessing. I clutch my hands into fists and lean forward, blowing the air out in a spiraling force from my lungs in the direction of the rats.

I'm sure the spell would have been far more catastrophic if I were full-sized, because wind rushes from my lungs and slams into the rats hard enough to blow them off their feet. They fly into the air and hit the ground several feet from where they were. This gives Tem enough time to reach me with Garrett, who is bleeding from four claw marks.

I reach out to fuss over him, but Garrett pushes my hand away. "Get back on Acorn. We still have to beat them to the door."

"Are you going to be all right, though?"

"It's a scratch." He climbs up behind me again. "Sorry about the quill, Acorn."

"You can make it up to me by bringing me more caterpillars when we get home." He takes off running again.

I glance over my shoulder and see that Garrett is also keeping an eye on the rats recovering and heading after us once again.

"We're almost to the door," Tem states from above.

"When we get there, you jump off and get under the door first," Garrett says. His tone is firm, and it's clear he's giving me a soldier's order. "I'll stand guard behind with the quill."

I want to object, but this is Garrett's element. This is what he was trained to do.

Acorn slows and stops much more gracefully when we reach the door. Garrett is instantly on his feet again and I drop down after him.

My heart pounds so loudly I'm grateful we are small and no one else can hear, unless they have some sort of supernatural ability to hear tiny heartbeats. Tem lies on his belly, opens his wings to make them flat, and scoots under. I follow his lead, lying down and pulling myself forward with my arms.

"Our dinner is getting away!" It's got to be one of the rats. Its voice is high and rattles.

Acorn tries to squeeze under next. Only, he gets stuck. "Oof!" he exclaims as he scratches his little nails against the stone, unable to get any sort of grip to help.

I grab one of Acorn's paws. "Come on, Acorn! Clearly I need to stop feeding you so much."

Acorn pouts. "I'm not fat."

"I'll push from behind!" Garrett says.

Acorn immediately starts to move, and I tug with all of my strength, pain etching through my shoulder.

When Tem grabs onto Acorn's other arm, he finally pops free and lets out a loud squeak when he does so.

"Did you hear that?" someone up the stairs asks.

I exchange a worried glance with Tem, who ushers me quickly to the far edge of the step, into the shadows. Garrett is immediately with us, and I can hear the rats scraping at the bottom of the door. We aren't completely hidden—the torches don't allow for complete darkness—but we might be lucky that they see the rats.

Luckily, Acorn is brilliant and hops up the first few steps on the side opposite where we stand.

"Ah. Of course you got out." The fairy descends the stairs.

I hold my breath.

The man crouches. His wings are blue, as is his hair, and he extends a hand to Acorn. "I warned you that it's dangerous being loose in the prison. Were the rats chasing you?"

"I was exploring," he answers, rather honestly, I might add. "And yes, the rats started chasing me!"

"It's dangerous in here, little one." He carries Acorn back up the stairs. "And not only because of the rats."

"I know. I like looking at the different creatures, though. And I wanted to see my friend again."

The fairy laughs and his voice fades away.

"Acorn is the best little creature," Garrett whispers.

Tem flies to the top of the stairs and leans around the corner, then motions us to go to the other side.

"How is your shoulder?" Garrett asks, clearly having noticed the grimace I tried to hide.

"There's something wrong. It hurts in a way that makes me fear it's not only an infection."

Worry pinches Garrett's brows. "I was afraid of that." He helps me up the last step.

The room is circular in shape, like the main entrance we were taken in through, but this place seems cozier. A glowing fireplace warms the room to the far left, a ladder is posted on the wall next to it, and tables and chairs fill the space. A bookshelf stands against the wall directly to our right that we easily slip behind. I peek around the shelves to see the fairy holding Acorn standing near the exit door. Most of the black-winged guards are eating their dinner. One is climbing the ladder.

"If we time this right, can we get out when he opens the door?" Garrett whispers.

It's not a short distance.

"If we use the table legs as shields, we can make it to the door. It's still dangerous. Be on your guard." Tem darts out to the nearest table.

I don't wait to be told to follow and press my back against the chair leg. I peer up at the guard at the next table.

Hiding beneath the table is easier than the chair, so I hurry under the nearby table just as Garrett has reached the first one.

"I was thinking you could let me out to eat," Acorn says. "All Elowyn had for me was a dead worm left over from the rainstorm yesterday. She tried to share her slop, but yuck."

The fairy guard chuckles. "I can let you outside." He opens the exterior door and steps outside.

"Behind him. Quick," Tem commands, pointing to the barrel beside the door.

I obey, sprinting across the open space and sliding behind the barrel. I'm breathing hard, my nerves starting to get the better of me. I know I have to wait for all of us to be in place to slip out together, or we risk one of us being seen.

Garrett takes his place at my side.

"Are there any wild animals nearby I need to know about?" Acorn asks. "Or can I just go hunt under any of the bushes?"

"I would avoid the pine tree at the far side of the road." The fairy points down the road. "There's a hawk there that enjoys rodents. Stay near this door."

My heart jumps. The opportunity couldn't be better.

Without a word being said to one another, we escape through the open door and take refuge in the nearest bush.

"Oh, thank you. I'll return in an hour," Acorn says.

The fairy guard steps back inside and closes the door behind him.

Acorn sniffs his way to us and proudly sits.

Garrett steps forward and rubs his nose. "You are brilliant."

I wrap my arms around his head. "I am so grateful you came on this adventure. Even if you're tired of it."

"Why, thank you. You would have all been in big trouble without me."

"You definitely saved the day," I agree.

Tem stretches. "Now all we have to do is make it to the main road and then through one of the portals."

"How long is this supposed to last?" Garrett asks.

I shake my head. "I don't know, to be honest. It could take us a couple of hours to return to our normal size."

Acorn heaves a heavy sigh. "Oh, great. We should make it to the main road by then, unless I carry you again."

"Riding you is very unpleasant," Garrett mutters. "I'd rather walk."

"And it would be good to stay alert and as quiet as possible," Tem says. "We don't want to draw the attention of predators."

"Like those?" Acorn points out.

I turn to see a set of green eyes disappear into the shadows. It appears escaping the prison hasn't provided much relief. Not only do we have to find a portal back to our realm, we have to do it while very small and unable to cover much ground. Oh, and with predators stalking us through the underbrush.

A rustle in the branches overhead steals my breath, but I can't see what it could be. My heart races—only for a nut to hit the ground and bounce.

"Ooh, a snack!" Acorn grabs it and makes quick work of the shell before devouring the nut.

"You're pretty loud for a creature of the night," Garrett mutters.

"Predators aren't so bad when you can spike them."

"Can you spike them and keep us safe at the same time?"

Acorn pauses, glances between us. "I'll keep Elowyn safe. You'll have to fend for yourself. Sorry, Whiskers."

I laugh. "It's good to know your priorities are straight." I lean forward and rub Acorn's head.

"He might switch alliances when I bring him a big jar of fat caterpillars," Garrett says.

"Ooh, that's tempting," Acorn replies.

A rabbit sprints across the trail in front of us, followed moments later by a larger shape I believe might be a fox, and my breath hitches. Right. Predators. No talking. We fall into tense silence as Acorn continues onward.

## Chapter Twenty

The sky's vibrant afternoon blue pales as the sun begins to shrink in the distance, and through the trees I see the lights of the fairy city begin to light. We've been walking for hours and Garrett had practically picked me up to ride Acorn when my shoulder started hurting again. Acorn travels between a quick waddle and brisk pace that Garrett is able to keep up with using long strides or a jog.

"Did we really get out without anyone noticing?" Garrett asks, glancing over his shoulder.

Tem flies alongside at our left so he can see us with his only eye. "The guards don't have an alarm they sound if something escapes. They don't want the people in the city terrified and causing more of a problem by overreacting."

"You don't warn them a dangerous creature might be headed their way?" He raises a brow.

"The soldiers are informed." Tem shrugs.

After a moment, I finally say something that has been on my mind. "I have a question about the binding."

"Yes?"

I shift, but there's no way to get comfortable. "What exactly did it do? I know it prevented fairies from crossing into our world, but Genoa was able to."

"Ah. Well, I assume Genoa was only able to cross through because of the Orbs of Olwar. Their power combined would be able to crack the barrier enough to let her through. She's mentioned doing so before, but she didn't know how. She must have figured it out."

"Now that it's gone entirely, what does that mean for the humans?"

Tem lands and walks alongside Garrett, though he's got to put a lot more effort into matching his stride as he's much shorter than Garrett. "A majority of the fairies aren't any more dangerous than a majority of humans. Genoa has . . . many loyal followers who will likely have joined her at Prince Kaison's castle."

"What's their aim?" Garrett asks.

"I don't actually know that," the fairy king replies. "She began entertaining ideas of taking over the throne to get revenge for being locked away and being denied our freedom for so many years. But taking the throne from the humans? And not all of them, just your country?" He shakes his head. "I spoke out and Nizra took my eye."

The blood in my veins freeze. "The eyes on Nizra's finger? One of them is yours?"

Tem nods.

I gag at the thought.

Tem continues, "I went to Genoa and pleaded with her to consider what this would do to our people. In return, she imprisoned me."

Garrett suddenly groans and places his hand on his chest.

"What's wrong?" I ask quickly.

But Garrett gasps before he is suddenly full-size again. He drops to his knees and gasps. "You need to work . . . on the transition part." He grimaces.

"I don't typically shrink living things like this," I reply. I climb off of Acorn to be sure that I don't accidentally harm him when transforming back myself.

A few moments later, we are all back to our normal sizes. Garrett hands me the pouch, which I shoulder and settle Acorn back inside of.

"You can rest all you want to," I say to him.

He grunts. "Yeah right. You're going to end up needing my help again, I just know it."

I roll my eyes with a smile and close the flap.

We're able to cross more ground now, and as the sun begins to finally set, a large, dark form begins to take shape. It stands out from the long shadows of the trees and short shadows of the bushes.

"This is the hat shop." I point at the metal sign nailed to the right side of the front door. "We're going through a door?"

"In Parshen?" Garrett asks.

"Yes. Entrance between our worlds is much easier than you must have believed."

I glance at Garrett. "We got through by stepping in a toadstool ring."

"Ah, the most ancient of passages." Tem walks around the front of the building to a door on its side. "Our portals between worlds are much easier now. They are simply doors. Enchanted, but doors nonetheless. This is the one we need. I have a feeling we are going to be getting a lot of curious visitors to our land over the next several days." He chuckles, then opens the door, revealing a shimmering surface with the distorted image of one of our streets.

"I'll go first," I offer.

"I'll follow," Garret says.

"I'll see you both on the other side," Tem says.

I step through the door only to exit out from a side door of the same hat shop in our land. The streets are dusted with a layer of snow and a brisk wind gusts, scattering snow from the roofs around to dance in the air.

"How is it already winter?" I mutter.

I glance around at the buildings and take specific note of the planter boxes hanging from the second stories of a few nearby buildings. One of the planter boxes hanging across the street from us filled with daisies and marigolds— which means it's supposed to be summer still. Their petals haven't browned yet, so the snow must have just begun and they didn't have a chance to encounter an autumn frost.

I wrap my arms around myself and turn back to the door. Garrett steps out, followed by Tem, and they join me in looking around at the snow.

"Hm. Her magic must be affecting the area," Tem ponders aloud. "Keep an eye out for anything out of the ordinary, just in case."

Acorn pokes his head out of the pocket. "Are we ready to break into the castle?"

I chuckle. "I think we need to be a bit careful."

Garrett's face falls. "I can't understand him anymore."

I look down at Acorn, who is scrambling to get out of the pouch. "You mean I can't talk to him and Kai anymore?" he asks.

"Easy!" I quickly grab him before he can fall to the ground.

Tem shakes his head. "Not in this realm, I'm afraid."

Acorn squeaks in dismay and lets me hold him. "I had a lot of fun teasing them, though!"

I hold him up to my face. "You'll just have to find other ways to tease." I kiss his nose and set him back in the pouch.

Garrett begins leading the way through the city and to the hill adorned by the castle. I never considered how strategic it was to place the castle there until I realize how exposed we are making our way up the road. But the slopes on either side are far too steep for us to scale, and we have no other choice than to be exposed.

Garrett has his attention locked on the walls. "Where are the guards?" he mutters.

My attention drifts to an eagle soaring overhead. "She

turned Kai into a frog. She may have turned them into animals. They would make much better spies."

Tem glances at me, then follows my gaze. "Perhaps. And if that is the case, she already knows we're here."

We reach the last bend and the gates stand open.

Garret pauses. He glances at me.

"What's that look for?" I ask.

He runs his tongue over his teeth, undoubtedly weighing all of his options. "I think you should go home and be safe."

I roll my eyes and cross my arms over my chest. "I've come all this way and you want to turn me around now?"

"Then I guess we enter through the front doors." Garrett sighs and steps forward carefully. "We don't have weapons to defend ourselves."

"I have a feeling it wouldn't matter if we did," Tem adds.

"Fair point." He grasps the handle of the door, looks at me, and then drags it open.

Genoa has converted the ballroom into a throne room, likely because her high throne of ice wouldn't fit in the throne room. Icicles have formed at the edges of the windows and on the chandeliers overhead. The king and queen sit to one side in brightly colored clothes with fake smiles plastered on their faces, looking like nothing more than human-sized dolls.

And Kai sits on another throne of ice, eyes frozen forward. He's in clean garments, now a beautiful shade of blue with green accents, and he has shaved his face and tied back his hair.

My heart aches when I see him. He should be fighting against her, running to me to make sure I'm all right. Instead, he doesn't even turn his head.

Genoa's laughter fills the hollow room. "You have the audacity to return? Even though I've already won?" She approaches us, but halts when her eyes drift from Garrett to Tem. Her smile slowly falls. "Temarilian. I thought I already got rid of you. Why can't you stay put?"

He steps between us, his movements slow, like he's approaching a wild animal. "Stars of my sky, I missed you. I came for you." He stops in front of her and carefully reaches out to stroke her cheek. "You still have color."

My breath catches and my heart skips.

Garret's shoulder bumps into me as he steps closer. I know what he wants to say without him uttering a word, because I think it too. Tem was on Genoa's side the entire time? As a partner?

Now we have to fight the fairy sorceress *and* the fairy king!

What spells can I utilize here?

"My love, you got what you wanted," Tem says softly. "The spell binding us to our realm is broken. We can now freely pass between realms. Isn't that enough?"

Her eyes, a cold gray-blue, narrow. "You never understood my desires."

"You can't have the human prince. You know this. You're married to me. *Bound* to me."

My gaze moves instantly to Kai.

Even though his body is rigid, his eyes slowly move to me and lock on. My heart is racing. Genoa is married to Tem? Does this mean . . . Kai isn't actually married?

*Get the other orb*, the hollow, ethereal voice of the orb whispers.

With Genoa distracted by her apparent *husband*, I take a cautious step toward the throne. The second orb lies on a pillar in the center of the room behind Genoa's back. I know I'm in her field of vision, so I move as slowly as I can in an effort not to draw attention. My lungs burn, begging for breath I hold inside.

"I want him. His kingdom will give us access to so much more!" Genoa says.

Tem takes her hands. "Do you not see what you've done to yourself?" He holds up her hand so she can see her long, sharp nails. "You're becoming darkness."

She jerks her hands away with a growl and waves a hand in the air in a circular motion. Ice crystals spiral in a circle before wrapping around Tem, squeezing his chest and lifting him from the ground. She flings her hand to the side, sending Tem flying through the air to collide with the wall high above the throne.

"Genoa!" he gasps. His wings are stretched outward from his body, and Genoa sends two icicles to pin his wings in place as collars of ice slide around his neck, wrists, and chest, all holding him to the wall.

Genoa laughs as she assesses her work. "This is rather fitting. Now you get to be on display here. Nizra should have done a better job keeping you contained. I'll have to punish him for failing me." She taps her chin.

With her back to me, I slip by and collect the orb from its resting place. All air is sucked from my lungs, and sparks shock through my fingers and across my tongue.

*We are reunited*, two voices say in unison. *Together forever, and never apart. Love brings power that shall not depart. Bound with love, strength in unison, resistance in trust.*

In a blink, I see a vision of Kai standing at my side in bright white clothes, our hands grasped, and light radiating from the two of us. Not only do I feel my own panic at Genoa's power and the revelation that Tem is her husband, but I also feel Kai's frustration that he can't move, his worry that I am about to be attacked by the sorceress. When our gazes meet, a tangle of emotions, strength, and fear threaten to overwhelm me.

*Give me to Prince Kaison,* the orb I've just lifted states. *I am not meant to be held by you. It draws confusion. Bring me to him.*

"Where was I?" Genoa claps her hands together and turns to face Garret. And me. Well, where I *should have* been. Instead, Garret stands alone, and I am now rather near her throne.

Without hesitation, I sprint toward Kai. Only, I feel my feet being dragged out from beneath me as Genoa uses a spell to pull me away. "Catch it!" I shout and throw the orb with all of my strength, not knowing if Kai even has the ability to move in order to catch it.

Genoa's magic is a gust of wind that sends me sliding back until I'm against the wall. My shoulder explodes in pain and I cry out.

Her lip curls in a smirk. "You've been bitten by darkness."

Behind her, Kai now holds the golden ball in his hands. Although he shudders, his gaze darts to Genoa and he slowly stands.

"Did you think that ball would give you more powerful magic?" Genoa asks. "Even though it is indeed a magical artifact, I'm afraid it doesn't work for just anyone." She stops directly in front of me. "This little bit of darkness . . ." She places her hand on my shoulder heavily. "It will slowly consume you if not stopped. But I should let it devour you so you can sit at my side, just as your poor lover does."

Garrett sprints forward.

Genoa's eyes dart to him and she reaches her hand out, then tightens it in a fist.

He gasps and drops to his knees, clutching his chest.

"Captain Garrett Bath, correct?"

Garrett struggles for breath.

"I believe you are due for a promotion. Colonel? Or perhaps even Constable?" She arches her brow. "You can have what you desire. All you have to do is swear your loyalty to me."

Garrett's blue eyes become hazy.

"No. Garrett, no!" I shout at him.

He blinks and shakes his head.

"Being a king's guard is honorable, certainly," Genoa says, her smooth voice slipping back into Garrett's ears. "But you've always wanted to prove your own worth. You've been nearly killed twice for the royal family. Isn't it time they respect that sacrifice?"

My throat goes dry. How can I possibly fight against a sorceress?

I slip my hand into my pouch and touch my mother's grimoire.

Genoa's attention snaps to me.

## Chapter Twenty-One

Genoa extends her hand to me. "Give me the grimoire."

An ache fills my bones, like I've swam too deep, and my ears feel like they're going to pop as she tries to use her magic to command me to obey. But I refuse to move. I won't let her control me.

"Stubborn little thing. Perhaps a rune of protection is hidden somewhere on you?" She leans to my ear. "Without the help of your little bodyguards, what can you possibly do against me?" Somehow, in the blink of an eye, she holds my mother's grimoire in her hand and tilts it forward and back.

"Give that back!" I attempt to snatch it from her, but she holds it up and just out of my reach.

"Ah-ah. This book may hold a lot of knowledge, but most importantly, it holds a tender place in your heart." She smiles like a viper.

Kai runs and reaches up to snatch the grimoire, but she wheels around and slams her palm against his chest. He rockets across the room, strikes the pillar the orb was on, and goes tumbling, dropping the orb and sending it rolling.

"Fools! All of you!" she snarls.

My heart slams against my ribs and I can barely

breathe. "Give. It. Back."

She clicks her tongue. "How could you be anything without this little book? What significant thing have you accomplished in your pathetic magical career? What would happen if it was . . ." She closes her hand into a fist, and fire ignites across the pages and envelops the cover.

"No!" I shout and snatch it from the air, but I have no choice but to drop it as the flames burn my palms. I cannot stop the flames from devouring it. All of my mother's knowledge, her years of failing and learning, trying and teaching, gone.

Gone.

Just like she is.

Genoa tilts her head back and laughs. A sound that should be light and filled with joy is dark and menacing.

I drop to my knees.

The pain in my hands pales in comparison to the pain in my heart. I've lost everything. Kai, Garrett, my mother, and now her knowledge. I really am nothing. I hold no value or worth to anyone.

"Kai, my darling husband. Come." Genoa drapes her hand in the air, fingers loose, arm extended toward Kai.

*My* Kai struggles to his hands and knees, and then to his feet. He's gritting his teeth, struggling to control himself.

"Genoa!" Tem calls. "Have you forgotten our marriage bond? Do you forget he cannot be your husband?"

She sneers and faces him. "I consider you dead to me,"

Genoa replies. "I can remarry if my spouse is dead."

Fear keeps my feet planted. I can't process what to do.

*Do spells have to be spoken? Genoa doesn't utter spells.* I can't tell if it's Kai's voice or the orb's.

I've never cast a spell without the incantation. I've never even created a rune without saying the words aloud. I know only those with incredible power and experience can use magic without speaking. Perhaps if I had listened to Kai and attended the university, I might be able to use those kinds of spells.

*Let Kai's strengths fill you,* the orb whispers through me. *What does he have that you can access?*

Kai is a soldier. Were it not for his gaze locked on mine, I would probably tremble with uncertainty. His brows shift and I can practically hear his voice tell me that I am brave too. But Kai has strength and determination I don't normally have, and the orb tells me I can access that. These characteristics provide a level of clarity to my mind I didn't know was possible. Instead of standing frozen in fear, I can think.

*Magic is part of you, like a thought.* That voice I know is the orb. *Use what is around you, Elowyn. You know how to do this.*

I look around the room.

Outside of the windows at the side of the throne room I can see wild valerian flowers, tiny white flowers on long green stems in clusters that are often mistaken for hemlock.

I know those can be used as a sleep aid, but I would have to get someone to sneak it into her drink. The flowers on the corner of the room are lilies of the valley, but I don't think there are enough that I could truly make her ill. And did I point out I don't have time or means to make potions?

My attention drifts back to the valerians, then dart to the sorceress.

I don't have to make her drink it. Maybe I just have to make her smell it?

Kai moves, snapping me back into the moment. He reaches a hand out toward the fireplace, where flames slowly lap at the logs beneath.

"What are you doing?" Genoa asks, her tone more curious than accusatory.

"The person I love has magic," he states. His gaze narrows on the flames as he concentrates, and suddenly flames burst from the fireplace and toward his hand. He lets out a startled yelp and flings the ball of fire at Tem, but luckily it hits the wall beneath the fairy.

Intentional or not, the heat causes the ice holding Tem to melt, and he drops to the ground. When he hits, there's a loud crunch like something has been broken.

Genoa growls. "Captain, get your weapon and stop the prince."

Garrett draws a sword from his hip that wasn't there previously and heads toward Kai with it poised.

Kai glances around for something to defend himself,

but he has no weapon and the only thing he can use would be an icicle.

It's time for me to stop worrying about everything that could go wrong. It's time to realize I am not a weak little forest witch who can only enchant with runes. I am a magic user capable of saving my kingdom from this insane fairy sorceress. If Kai can use the power of the orb to access my magic and grab a fireball, I have the ability to use more power than I thought possible.

As Garrett engages Kai with the sword, Kai ducks and drives his elbow into Garrett's ribs.

Genoa turns to me.

My blood runs cold.

But I don't have time to linger in fear as her hand closes into a fist and sparks ignite around it before a bolt of lightning flies toward me.

My mind can only process two thoughts: deflect it, or grab it. Luckily for me, my hands react before I fully process what is happening—and apparently my brain has chosen to snatch the lightning. The crackling heat envelops my hands and dances between my fingers. I feel sluggish as I turn and throw the ball back at her with both hands, releasing the lightning with as much energy as I can muster. The sensation of magic tingling through me exhales like I've been diving beneath water.

The bolt strikes Genoa's shoulder when she tries to dodge it. It barely seems to faze her as she doesn't even hesitate before casting her next spell, a flurry of ice daggers.

I step toward the fireplace and, like Kai, take the flames and pull them in front of me, using the heat as a shield. As the ice hits the flame, it melts, which puts out the fire and fills the room with black smoke.

I hear Garrett or Kai grunting, and then one of them shouts in pain. A sword clatters and someone growls.

Using the smokescreen to my advantage, I hurry to my right, my hand out. I know the wall is somewhere this way and all I want to do is get some space between myself and Genoa.

*I am clever and resourceful*, I tell myself as I fish out the golden ball from the pouch. "You are the orb that was used to turn Kai."

*Yes.*

"Show me the enchantment she used."

*Clever girl.* I vividly see the runes Genoa used spread across its surface.

Almost instantly, the smoke in the room clears as Genoa casts a spell to blow wind through it.

My heart leaps as realization hits me. "There isn't just one rune!"

I've used runes my entire life. But never have I seen them combined to create a spell or enchantment. I've used them to heal, to repel bugs, and to shrink things, and they're such a basic form of magic that almost anyone with the tiniest bit of magic can use them. But there are more to runes than basic enchantment. I learned that a long time ago. The smallest twist on the edge of a line can change the entire meaning of the rune.

And now I know they can be used together to create something more powerful.

I may not be able to read the fairy's runes and understand what spell *she* used. But I don't need to.

I quickly look up as a figure runs toward me, and I see Kai slide on his knees to my side. "What are you doing?" he asks. He grips his ribs and Garrett is sprawled on his back, dazed and blinking at the ceiling.

"I'm going to use Genoa's spell against her. I need you to distract her. Watch out!" I grab Kai and pull him down, narrowly missing an arrow of ice.

He lands on top of me, somehow supporting himself on his forearms instead of landing with all of his weight on my chest. It would be romantic, being this close to him, if it weren't for the sorceress already calling upon another spell to kill us in the background.

"Whatever you're going to do, do it fast." Kai pushes himself up and runs at Genoa.

I wish I had time to dwell on how handsome he is, how brave, and how good he smells. But I roll up to my knees and focus all of my attention on the golden orb in my hands.

"Oof!" Kai goes flying past me, sliding on his back across the ground.

My mind quickly races for what runes to call upon. *Re*

*hume, re ezdna, let ruendin* is the spell for shrinking. I don't necessarily need the entire spell, just the *ezdna*, for the size, and *ruendin*, which creates the rune itself. If I change *hume* to . . . *ellidian* that would be the proper word for small animal, but I could even be more specific with . . . *moroshin*? No, *amphaudin*. *Audin* is the rune for life, and *amph* should be enough to make her a frog.

"Get back on your feet!" Genoa commands. I glance up to see Garrett fumbling to his feet, but Kai throws broken icicles at Genoa purely as a distraction.

I don't have time to ask for confirmation before I cast the spell, and I barely have enough time to quickly etch the three runes on the dirt ground. It's far from ideal. I can barely make them out, and I know there is significant risk in rushing it, but I have no choice.

Heat scorches my right ear and I lean away in a flinch. I look over to see Kai duck out of the way behind his mother's throne as the fireball slams into the wall where he just was.

Our gazes lock.

I quickly say, "*Re amphaudin, re ezdna, let ruendin.*" The sensation of magic rests in my sternum like a buzz of excitement.

The fireball aimed at Kai is quickly followed by a gust of wind, which slams into me, but the words have been spoken. Luckily, I'm kneeling on the floor and the wind only has the strength to blow me backward instead of sending me rolling. To my amazement, the runes float into the air and settle on the orb. The instant they touch, their color changes to orange.

She faces me, her expression contorted into nothing less than a monster.

The orb is slowly rolling in her direction.

Her teeth are fangs, her wings gray, and her complexion pale. "The orb! How dare you try to steal it!" she screeches.

I make like I'm trying to reach it before her, but with her wings she's much faster than I am. She snatches it from the ground, wheels around, and flings her hand at me. Icicles sting my face, which I shield with my forearm. Dazed, I blink through the bright white light in my vision and finally focus on the icy prison surrounding me, pinning me against one of the floor-to-ceiling stained-glass windows.

Through the pillars of ice, I watch a warm glow of light slowly enveloping Genoa.

"What have you done?" she demands, shaking her hands and looking down at her arms. In a flickering image, Genoa's fairy form fades in size and shape from her arms to her legs until she has become nothing but a frog. "You turned me into a frog?" she screams.

Garrett staggers, his sword stopping mid-blow as Kai rolls away. His eyes are back to normal and he has a bruise already forming on his jaw. "What . . . happened?" he asks through deep breaths.

Kai faces me. "How was that supposed to help? I thought you were going to kill her!"

"I don't kill things!" I shout back.

"Can't she just reverse the spell with her magic?" Kai asks.

I stare up at him. That . . . had actually not occurred to me. She created her original spell, and any good sorceress would have come up with the counter spell for this very spell just in case she accidentally touched it and needed to turn herself back, which means at any moment she could return to being a fairy.

Tem crawls out from the icy throne, looking awful and bleeding from his head. I'd forgotten all about him. "She needs . . . to use . . . light magic." He winces. "She needs to get outside."

"Then catch her!" I yell at Kai, pushing with all my weight against the ice to try to break it.

Garrett, still dazed, staggers and reaches for the hopping frog headed for the front door.

"Oh, no you don't!" Kai says and runs after her.

With the effort of unfamiliar magic sapping my strength, I barely have the energy to push against the ice, let alone use another spell. But I have to stop Genoa. I have to help them catch her before she can reverse the spell. With the little strength I have, I draw the fire one last time from the fireplace to melt one pillar just enough for me to slip out of my prison.

I stumble through the open front doors of the castle in time to see Kai dive for the frog. But without warning, without even a sound, a hawk dives from the tree and plucks her from the ground.

"That's not a frog!" I shout in horror.

But the hawk refuses to listen. He lands on a branch and tears into Genoa.

I clamp both hands over my mouth.

Kai slowly gets to his feet, eyes wide and face pale. "That . . . that could have been me." He gulps and slowly faces me. "I could have . . . died that night." He closes the gap between us and draws me into his arms. "You saved me. Not only that night, but just now." He holds me tightly. "Elowyn. I don't deserve someone as good as you."

I laugh, too tired to consider a different reaction, and lean into him. "And I didn't even attend university."

That draws a choked laugh from Kai, and he loosens his grip.

"Tem . . ." I pull away from Kai and rush back inside.

Tem leans against the wall with Garrett now tending to him.

"I am so sorry," I blurt to the fairy.

His eye is sad and he nods solemnly. "I knew she was gone when she saw me. She was beyond saving. Cruel fates befall the cruel."

I bite my bottom lip.

Kai hugs me from behind and pulls me tightly to him. "I knew you could do it," he says, his breath brushing my ear.

"That makes one of us."

He chuckles and turns me to face him. His eyes draw me in and shine with pride. I don't know why my heart swells so much. Mother always expressed her pride in me, but seeing Kai acknowledge my abilities and love me for them brings tears to my eyes. I've fought for so long to feel wanted and needed, and here it is in Kai's arms.

"Is it true?" he asks tentatively.

"What?" I ask.

Kai looks at Tem. "Is it true I'm not married to Genoa?"

"She's dead now, so it wouldn't matter. But no. You were never legally married. The orbs connected to the two of you because of your true love for one another. Her orb connected to you, Elowyn. Maybe the other orb attached to Kai, but because the two of you hadn't admitted your feelings, they couldn't really reach you."

Kai's eyes light up.

I cannot resist my own rush of excitement.

"Elowyn." He cups my face in his hands. "I love you. I always have."

My chest clenches. "Kai . . ." I swallow hard. "I love you too." I crush my lips to his.

He wraps his arms around my shoulders and slides one hand down to my lower back. I slip my hands up his muscled back and hold on while his lips caress mine. His warm breath caresses my cheek while his lips caress mine. The kisses travel down my jaw to my neck. My fingers grip his shirt and I press as tightly to his body as possible.

We fit together like a puzzle, and a piece of my heart has been returned to its rightful place. I should have forgiven him long ago. As his lips claim mine again, I adjust my hold so my fingers tangle in his black hair.

I settle on my feet, my heart pounding so hard against my ribs my chest might explode. And I don't care if it does.

He smiles and strokes his knuckles across my cheek. "You are the most beautiful person I've ever known. Will you be my wife?"

I laugh and wrap my arms around his neck and kiss him again, then mutter over his lips, "Do you even need to ask?"

He chuckles, vibrating my lips. "Is that yes?"

I look into his beautiful eyes. "Yes."

I am finally where I belong.

## Chapter Twenty-Two

The aftermath of Genoa is difficult for Kai. We re-enter the castle to find his parents alert and appearing rather exhausted. Kai holds my hand and stops in front of them. With my connection with him through the orbs, I sense his flurry of emotions, from relief his parents are alive, to resolution on whatever decision he has made.

"Kaison," his father begins.

But Kai holds up his hand. "I know the truth. Genoa told me everything, and King Temarilian confirmed it all." He glances in the direction of the injured fairy.

Garrett has bandaged his arm, somehow having already retrieved a medicine kit.

"I fought my entire life to prove myself to you. To be what you wanted," Kai continues. "No more. I will marry Elowyn, as my marriage to Genoa was not legally binding."

"And she's dead," I mutter.

He rubs his thumb against the back of my hand. "And I'm taking the throne," he says firmly.

King Willard's mouth moves in a fluster of emotions, though no words come out for a moment. "Kaison, please think reasonably. I am still the king. You have been through a lot recently and—"

"This isn't up for negotiation." He turns to his mother. "I'll allow you and Father to stay in the summer cottage. You'll still have your needs met. I met your demands of marriage and you will resign the throne to me. Maybe someday in the future we can have more of a discussion, but not now."

"I'm sorry," his mother whispers. "We should have told you."

He nods. "You should have." He turns away and retreats to help take care of Tem.

I awkwardly follow, glancing at the king and queen, whose eyes are filled with tears. It's their own fault they've pushed Kai away like this.

Over the next several days, doctors are called to tend to Tem, Kai works with his political men in the castle to get things in order for his coronation, and Garrett checks in with the soldiers.

A few days after the chaos begins to settle, Tem reveals Kai is actually legally a fairy prince too.

"What?" Kai asks, staring down at Tem, who is sitting in a rocking chair in the castle gardens.

Tem sighs. "Because of the arrangement between our worlds, you are legally a prince. The arrangement was for you to be our child, and to the fairy people you are the kidnapped fairy prince."

Kai runs his fingers through his hair. "I don't want to be

a prince of the fairy realm."

Tem smiles. "I'm afraid it's not really a role you can step out of any more than you could step out of your role as prince here."

"I have enough to be concerned about in my own kingdom right now. How can I possibly step in and help run your kingdom?"

"You don't have to," I offer.

He looks sideways at me.

"When Tem heals, you can send him home and back to his throne." I step up to Kai's side and take his hand. "You can meet the people, but you don't need to take on their responsibilities too.

"In the meantime, I can write decrees letting our people know they aren't in danger." Kai nods. "I'll let the fairies know our borders are open again."

After helping clean up the flooded throne room after all of Genoa's ice melts, I return to my cottage just to check on things and properly wash up. I find Pancho has found his way home and is grazing merrily in the meadow near the barn, which brings me relief.

"Pancho!" I call to him.

He lifts his head and snorts. "You left."

I run and hug him around the neck. "I'm so grateful you're safe. Did you get hurt by the troll?" I step back to assess him for injury. Luckily, he has none.

"Phil wants to go home."

"Phil?" I gasp. "Garrett's horse!" Leaving Pancho behind, I hurry to the barn and open the stall door. "I completely forgot about you! I'm so sorry!"

"I had enough food," the horse replies. "I am rather bored, though."

"I was just going to wash up and return to the castle. You can go with me, if you'd like," I offer.

"I would like that very much."

I reach out and rub his velvet nose. "You can drink from the stream and munch on whatever weeds you wish. I'll return as quickly as I can."

When I do, the horse, whose name is Phil, invites me to ride on his back to the castle.

Days later, the hot air is so humid, my tunic sticks to me. I wore a dress yesterday and was so miserable I hoped pants and a tunic would be cooler today. It's rather the opposite, and my fingers sting from pulling out so many weeds and transplanting bulbs and plants from my garden into pots. Every now and then my shoulder burns with movement, but the bite mark and black veins are almost completely gone.

Kai pulls his shirt off and tosses it over the fence, revealing the muscles of his finely toned body. "I can't believe you're having me pull weeds the day before our wedding." He smiles playfully.

I've seen him without his shirt dozens of times. We've gone swimming, changed after being muddy, and warmed up under the blankets after a day in the snow. Of course, I've never been down to less than my chemise or nightgown.

Today, I see him differently.

He is a man, his arms flexing as he digs his fingers into the soil to lift out the halavase I've asked him to retrieve. The muscles of his back ripple under his sweat, and I cannot help but stare at every inch of his exposed torso. "You're distracted," he comments.

When I meet his gaze, he's smiling proudly.

"You took your shirt off on purpose," I say and settle the halavase into a small terracotta pot.

"Of course I did." He chuckles.

"You should not be doing such things when I'm busy."

"Do you find me irresistible?" I feel him crouch at my side, and his breath whispers down my neck and across my cheek.

"Distracting," I correct.

He places his hand on my cheek and turns my face to him so he can plant his lips on mine. I don't mind the roughness of his muddy hand when I have the tenderness of his lips against mine. "You like my distraction," he says against my lips.

"I suppose so." I smile and wink. "Get back to work. I'm not doing this all on my own."

He laughs. "That should be your next enchantment. Getting rid of weeds!"

I nudge him with my shoulder just hard enough to make

him tip pack on his ankles. "I thought this was your favorite pastime?"

"Spending time with you, always. This?" He shrugs. His gaze drifts and he stands. "Garrett is headed this way." Kai tilts his chin down to point with his head, as his hands are occupied with clusters of weeds he has just gathered.

"What are you doing?" I call to Garrett as I stand, dusting my hands on my pants.

He is in less formal clothing than his uniform, though he still wears his cloak with the royal pin, and he rides on his beautiful horse, Phil. Garrett's face is clean shaven, save his familiar mustache, though it is trimmed and in perfect shape.

He raises his hand in greeting. "I owe Acorn caterpillars," he calls back.

I laugh. "He's going to be thrilled! He's been getting worms for two days." I hold up a writhing worm in my hand. "Mother, will you bring Acorn out?"

My mother exits our cottage with Acorn in her hands. She still has her smile. Although her hair was shorn to her shoulders, it looks nice on her. She's got more gray at her temples than I remember, but her brown and lavender eyes are still filled with the same bright light as always. "Good day, Captain Bath."

Garrett shakes his head. "No formalities required, ma'am. Just Garrett."

"And yet you call me ma'am like an old lady?" Mother

responds.

We all smile.

Garrett rubs the back of his neck. "I've never called a woman by her name."

"What do you think I am?" I ask.

His eyes widen. "That's not what I meant! I meant . . . uh . . ."

Kai laughs and nudges Garrett with his elbow, his hands still covered in mud. "Garrett, they're playing with you. Best stop before you offend either one, hm?"

He clears his throat. "Right. I see where Elowyn gets it, though."

Kai twitches his brows. "Indeed. El, give me your weeds." He crosses his arms so I can add my weeds into his arms. He then turns and walks to the pile of weeds that have been accumulating at the far end of the garden.

"Are you going somewhere?" I ask Garrett, pointing out the packs on his horse's saddle. I reach up to pat Phil's neck.

Garrett slips down and lands on the ground. "It turns out unlocking the fairy realm has allowed fairies and humans to cross back and forth." He raises his brows, as that is something we had discussed some time ago. "Tem knows a fairy king with twelve daughters who seem to go missing each night. He's asked for help uncovering where they are going and what they're doing. Because Prince Kaison's now royalty between the two realms, he has offered my assistance."

"Twelve?" I raise my brows. "That's good odds for you."

He rolls his eyes. "I think Kai is trying to make it up to me, because I'm positive they can solve this terrible mystery on their own if they tried."

"The king agreed to let you marry one if you can figure out what's happening," Kai adds as he rejoins us. "I fail to see how that could be anything but good for you."

I can no longer hold back my laugh.

Garrett smiles but shakes his head. "I'm not that desperate."

"Whiskers!" Acorn squeaks as he wakes.

I translate for Garrett, and the soldier leans down to rub Acorn's nose. "I brought you the caterpillars I promised. It turns out the gardens of the castle have quite a bit more variety than I imagined." He withdraws a jar from his pocket with five or so plump caterpillars, and all are a variety of colors.

"Ooh! I do like the monarch caterpillars. They're sweet. Eww. Fuzzy ones?"

"I thought that would be fun for you," Garrett replies after I again translate.

Acorn frowns. "Have you ever tried to eat something fuzzy?"

I tilt my head. "Considering he has one under his nose, I would say yes."

"One what?" Garrett asks.

Acorn giggles and reaches his hands out. "Tell him

thank you. Is he going to be gone long? Maybe next time he can take me to the castle so I can search the gardens myself."

I smile as Garrett sets the jar of caterpillars in Mother's hands beside the hedgehog. "Acorn would like you to take him through the castle gardens sometime when you get back."

"I would like that." He smiles. "Aren't you going to be there though?"

I nod and smile at Kai. "That doesn't mean Acorn won't want your attention any less, though. I believe he feels a bit bored lately."

Acorn scoffs. "I am fine not going on an adventure for a very long time. I'll stay here with your mother to keep the garden clear of pests. Going with you might mean more unnecessary danger."

I laugh and turn back to Garrett. I pull him into a hug. "I wish you all the best, Whiskers."

He chuckles, the sound radiating in my head, and then steps back. He looks at Kai. "Good luck with this one. She's going to keep you on your toes."

Kai shakes Garrett's hand and then slides his arm around my waist. "Good luck, Constable."

Garrett waves his hand dismissively, turns, and mounts his horse.

"Wait! I want to give you something." I hurry back into the cottage to retrieve the waterskin we brought back from the prison. I take it back outside and hold it up to him.

"What's this?" he asks as he accepts it.

"A parting gift. I've been practicing my runes." I point to the etching in the leather. "This is a waterskin that will never run dry."

Garrett's brows lift in an impressed look. "Wow. That's valuable."

"After the situation with the prison, I knew something like this would be important."

"You made this for me before you knew I was leaving?"

I nod. "It doesn't matter where you're going, I know you're always traveling."

"Thanks. Thank you, Elowyn." He slips the strap over his head, then waves one last time and begins down the path to the main road.

"Why did you really send him to find a bunch of princesses?" I ask Kai.

"One of them is bound to love him." He grins.

"I've got tea and coffee and some lunch ready," Mother says as she turns back to our cottage.

Kai turns with me. "When does Professor Alice come for your lessons?"

"Tomorrow." I step into my cottage and can't help but feel my heart swell.

Mother has a lovely spread across the counter with summer berries in a bowl, a pound cake, and sandwiches.

I wash my hands in the sink beside Kai, then take a small handful of blueberries and pop two in my mouth.

Everything is as it should be.

Mother is home, Acorn is sleeping in his burrow on the counter, and Kai is at my side teasing me about the state of my workbench. I'm not annoyed at all. For once, I find it terribly endearing. I nearly lost him. I nearly lost all of this. I will never take my ordinary day for granted again.

Unless it involves weeding.

# The End

More adventures to come in the new series,
*Sisters of the Briar*.

# About Me:

*Personal dragon trainer, lover of glitter, writer of fantasy.*

Reading has always been a huge passion of mine. From being swept away with a giant at night to riding dragons, I love the escape that comes with a good book. Some of my fondest memories are at the library!

With a background and multiple degrees in education, I believe books should represent people with all abilities and invite the reader to consider different perspectives on life. I also write books with no damsels in distress.

I currently live in Salt Lake City, UT with my adorable King Charles Spaniels, Perseus and Ollivander, and work full-time as a kindergarten teacher.

I am a USA Today Bestselling author and have been nominated for various awards, including "Unforgettable Book of the Year."

**Join my reader group on Facebook:**
**Lichelle's Book Wyrms**

# Dear Reader,

I hope you enjoyed reading this story as much as I enjoyed creating it. I truly grew to love Garrett and couldn't just let him go without receiving his own happily ever after, could I? You'll see him again in my retelling of Rose Red!

- Chapter 8 - When Elowyn is sharing how Samuel used to call her a troll, this is a nod to my dear grandmother, Pamela Burke. She told me a story of how her dad used to call her mom his little "troll," which in Sweden is meant as a term of endearment.

- Chapter 13 - When Nizra says, "We only bite on Thursdays. Is today Thursday?" this is in reference to something I say frequently when people are looking for somewhere to sit. I will invite them over and say, "I only bite on Thursdays." One day I said this it happened to be Thursday. We had a good laugh and became instant friends.

- Chapter 16 - Yes, the reference to the pouch being "bigger on the inside" is a direct reference to Doctor Who. I fell in love with the show with David Tennant as the Doctor.

Sign up for my newsletter at: LichelleSlater.com

*(Find me on Instagram, Facebook, and more!)*

# ALSO BY LICHELLE SLATER

## *Fairytale Retellings*
### *THE FORGOTTEN KINGDOM*
**The Four Stones of Tern Tovan**
(Prequel)
**The Dragon Princess**
(Sleeping Beauty Reimagined)
**The Siren Princess**
(Little Mermaid Reimagined)
**The Beast Princess**
(Beauty and the Beast Reimagined)
**The Phoenix Princess**
(Snow White Reimagined)
**The Crown Prince**


### *SANDS OF WONDER*
**The Sultan and The Storyteller**
(Prequel and currently part of *A Villain's Ever After*)
**Daughter of Thieves**
**Guardian of Thieves**


### *SISTERS OF THE BRIAR*


## *Epic Fantasy*
### *A Plague of Magic*
**Beyond the Outer Wall**

## Science Fiction/Fantasy:

### CIRCUS OF THE STARS
Ringmaster
Marionette
Magician

## Urban Fantasy:
Curse of a Djinn

## Christmas:

### CHRISTMAS ROMANCE NOVELS
Secret Santa
Accidental Secret Santa